The Memoirs of

Caesar Honore

A Curious Enterprise in the
Gold Fields of California in 1849

Annotated by his Grandson
Bayard Taylor Honore, Jr.

Eugene L. Conrotto

HypatiaMedia.com

elc@hypatiamedia.com

Dedication

This book is for

Dan Langhoff

...my student who became my teacher

— E.L.C.

Contents

Dedication..iii

A Forenote.. vi

In The Beginning.. 1

Judge Milton's Court.. 18

On to Monterey... 32

The Vista Del Mar... 47

Introducing the Cast... 52

A Flurry of Activity... 57

Reenter Billy Tremaine.. 61

On Bayard Taylor..66

Trapping Zachary Fenner.. 70

Finishing Up in Monterey..75

John C. Fremont.. 80

Doc and Phiggy.. 86

Companions..90

We Start for the Great Central Valley.. 91

Pairings..93

Burgundia (1)..97

Burgundia (2)..101

Milford "Doc" Brewer, Ole Bull,and Our "Decameron"..... 102

Over the Pacheco Pass..110

The California Constitutional Convention Ends...................114

Joaquin...116

Trouble With the "Law"... 120

In the Foothills...123

Burgundia's Letter.. 126

Indian Friends..128

Sonoran Camp (1)... 131

Sonoran Camp (2)... 137

A Summons from Hyrum...140

Zachary Fenner's Bees...142

Life in Sonora...147

Burgundia... 152

Civic Violence...154

Daphne and Billy.. 162

Fenner Turns Up in Sonora... 165

Wrapping Up Business..169

About the Author..173

Afterword...174

A Forenote

I shall refer to my grandfather in these notes as "C.H." I do this not out of lack of affection or to save printer's ink, but as a reminder to me that the annotator's posture should be one of objectivity. C.H. was not a man with whom one—especially a worshipping grandson—could be objective. If love finds its way into this text, then I beg the reader to give me the benefit of the doubt and assume that love is a fitting supplement to the note at hand.

— Bayard Taylor Honore Jr.

What do we want with this vast, worthless area? This region of savages and wild beasts, of deserts of shifting sands and whirlwinds of dust, of cactus and prairie dogs? To what use could we ever hope to put these great deserts, or those endless mountain ranges, impenetrable and covered to their very base with eternal snow? What can we ever hope to do with the western coast, a coast of three thousand miles, rock-bound, cheerless, uninviting, and not a harbor on it? What use have we for this country?

— Daniel Webster [1]

[1] C.H. saw Webster when the Senator was guest-of-honor at the Godfrey Lawrence Latin Academy in Boston. C.H. was eight and in the lower form, although he was a front bench scholar. He often told the story of his "brush with greatness," especially when one of his grandchildren showed prejudice toward an exotic dish at table. Webster was what the Italians label "a great fork," but at the Lawrence School outing he was rather picky. Headmaster Lawrence had asked mothers of his scholars to prepare "delicacies" for the great man. My great-grandmother Carolina sent a plate of ravioli in a rich sauce whose chief ingredient was the flesh and bones of 16 sparrows, C.H. knowing the exact number because he had trapped them and had the opportunity to re-check his figures when it became time to pluck the birds. Webster not only did he not sample Mama's ravioli-con-passero, he took time out of his busy schedule to laud "Plain Yankee cooking" when scooping up a mess of plain Yankee porridge. This—plus Webster's betrayal to his constituents by supporting the Fugitive Slave Act, telling Massachusetts in the process to conquer her "prejudice" regarding the Southern slavers, that compromise was necessary to save the Union—relegated the Senator to a class of politicians whom C.H. called "Pis-ants." There is no doubt in my mind that C.H. used Webster's "prejudice" against California and the West as an introduction to his memoirs was done so to satisfy the human appetite for revenge. What better way to hang a man than by his own words? What better way to erase the hurt of an eight-year-old having to stand in front of his eager-to-hear mother inquiring about Webster's reaction to her raviolis? "The Senator loved your ravioli, Mama," said the lad wise beyond his years in the art of diplomacy. "The big pig ate them all!"

1

In The Beginning...

San Francisco, 1912 [2]

Biography is the only true history [3]

During my long life I have done little, but have done so with a great deal of skill. The opportunity to live long and to do little came from the exciting and unusual job of work I performed during my twentieth and twenty-first years. That adventure is the subject of this chronicle.

In youth we feel riches for every new illusion; in mature years for every one we lose.[4]

Foul-smelling and impatient Death, hopping from one foot to the other, may cause me to pause over-long over memories of California and youth, for it came to me in a dream that I would not die until this work was completed. For this I beg your indulgence.

I entered into the singular adventure which occupied those long-ago days, with a desire to get on in the world. To do so one must keep eyes and ears open, and mouth shut. The young man without means who yearns to succeed must, in

---

[2] This is the place and year of C.H.'s death.

[3] This quote is from Carlyle. Emerson: "There is properly no history, only biography."

[4] A quote—without acknowledgement—to Mme. Swetehine. As Goethe writes, there would be little left of him if he were to discard what he owed to others.

addition, give his employer absolute loyalty. And always remember that strangers and rogues often give the best advice.[5] And that it is lawful to be taught by an enemy.[6]

I was born on July 8, 1829, in Boston, Massachusetts, the only child of Enrico and Carolina Honore, British subjects of Piedmontese origin. My parents made their way north through Europe,[7] and then west across the turbulent Atlantic as manservant and maid to Lord Hector John-Cowe.[8] "We serve and he pays," is the way my mother described her station in life. "He's English," she would add with a shrug that conveyed all that had to be passed-on by way of additional dialog.

John-Cowe, a representative of his family's banking house,[9] had no trouble making the clever Italian couple citizens of his country. It took but one letter and with it complications of origins and frontiers vanished. One letter — and my parents, and I, came in possession of the most valuable piece of paper on earth: a British passport.

"You see," said the Lord, "you're now bloody British despite those God-damnable head-kerchiefs and baggy trousers you insist on wearing." My parents remained

---

[5] This business of strangers and rogues giving the best advice is lifted from C. H. Bailey, and often quoted by C.H. His home was overrun by such persons — all were welcome: saint or sinner.

[6] The quote here is lifted from Cicero or Seneca. C.H. had a penchant for things Roman.

[7] John-Cowe engaged my great-grandparents during his year-long stay in Savonna in 1827. He then returned briefly to London, and departed for New York and Boston on March 15, 1828. My great-grandparents were in his service a total of 22 years. John-Cowe never married, upon his death left $10,000 to Enrico and Carolina. The bulk of his estate went to various nephews, some of whom I met in San Francisco banking circles.

[8] Actually, they were a bit more than that. Enrico kept the Lord's books and was, in fact, his private secretary, for John-Cowe made these various forays into remote parts of the globe not so much as to find recreation as it was to check-up on his family's financial interests. Carolina took on the manservice duties: she fed, clothed and groomed John-Cowe.

[9] Pinder's Trust. The wealth flowed down from the mother's side. The bank failed in the panic of 1893.

themselves in dress and soul whenever they were not acting for John-Cowe in some official capacity. They only half-trusted what they could see of English ways in London and of American ways in Boston, and, finally, in California, only half-trusted in God.

John-Cowe, for reasons known only to himself, his family, and, no doubt, to a few others in England, spent the entire second half of his life away from his mother country. The particular skeleton in his closet was no doubt a moldy one. There were hints — mostly from my mother's rolling eyes — that John-Cowe favored boys and in time I began to understand why it was I never found myself alone in John-Cowe's company.

John-Cowe to my knowledge never once referred to America by its given name. It was always the "bastard states." "Only good thing about this God-damnable country is your beef. It's not particularly fine beef, but there's so God-damnably so much of it."[10]

Looking back I am more inclined to think John-Cowe's major deficiency was not gluttony or sodomy but rather dullness. The trouble with that unclassified venal sin is that it is catching, and my parents strove mightily to keep this disease at bay. They did this by reading aloud to one another, and as soon as I was able to understand some of the "big words," included me in this brand of group therapy.[11]

---

[10] John-Cowe must have held some sort of record in this category. C.H. suggested that John-Cowe had better pray God is not a cow because God's punishment will make Hell's lakes of fire seem like a pleasant afternoon at the Sutro Baths. John-Cowe liked his beef boiled. Upon huge mounds of meat he would pour either a green (parsley, onions, garlic, olive oil) or red (garlic, bell pepper, tomato) *bagno* — "bath." This is how C.H. ate, and how even to the generation of my grandchildren ate beef.

So much for acquired taste.

[11] My birthday and Christmas gifts from C.H. were always books, and with each book a fancy or unusual pen or pencil, to remind me to write in the book margins, to ask questions, to challenge, to underscore, in short to participate with the author in his or her search for truth or beauty or nothing at all.

Aside from my nightly rendezvous with my family reading circle, my boyhood environment was not stimulating. Boston had its great port, and its ships brought exciting cargo from the far corners of the world, but I saw little of this nor was I touched by much of it. An occasional Feejee Islander or a hairy Bantu with a monkey perched on his shoulder would cross my path on my way to or from school or on an emergency errand to fetch a spool of white thread, but there was no conversation, no gaining of insight as to why the Feejee sailor covered his walnut skin with eggplant-purple tattoos, or why the Hairy Bantu allowed a wild, agitated, constantly chattering monkey shit all down his back.

And as I passed through adolescence and the forces of nature took over, demanding night and day that I fulfill my mission in the great scheme of creation to add new souls to the population, my curiosity centered on the great mystery of life, to wit, why did my male peers mock the Feejee Sailor and the Bantu Shit-back, while my female peers could not hide a slight flare of their nostrils when reflecting on our visitors from abroad?

John-Cowe was not an evil or spiteful man. He simply was unfeeling. On our trip around the Horn to California he had two score pieces of luggage; 5000 silver dollars; a manservant and his wife and their son—in short 5042 separate and distinct possessions. His watery-blue eyes and smooth brick-red face held but one message: disdain. Poor man. He had nothing to be disdainful about. His fat fingers told his entire, wasted story.

I recall him worse (with the sharpness that bitterness gives the senses) during our cold, horrible passage to San Francisco. He was sitting in the saloon, his massive back steadying the root of the great mast, a human sack of sawdust, forking food into his mouth while the very sight of vittles made me and everyone else on the ship desperately ill. His enormous belches caused the ship's confused seasick rats to give up their safe berths and scurry to find another. And when John-

Cowe broke wind one of our fellow emigrants cried out, "The sails are rend in twain!" To which John-Cowe roared back: "What fool of a passenger would think sails would be shown in such a storm?"

My mother left us with the final verdict on John-Cowe's gastro-intestine prowess: "He's the only man whose farts cause me to pray." Because of this sea outing, I never again set foot on a floating plank.[12]

The clipper ship *Tronka*[13] passed through California's Golden Gate on August 5, 1849 — a date otherwise made famous in Yerba Buena[14] for the fact the Baptists of this city dedicated the first Protestant Church in California on that day.

When a skiff pulled up alongside the *Tronka*, I grabbed my purse, told my folks I would meet up with them later, jumped aboard, grabbed an oar, and with oar and determination caused that skiff to literally fly across the water.

On that very first moment on dry land I was reborn, despite my India rubber legs. I wanted to pound those legs into the sandy soil, to reach up and fly with the gulls, to shout

---

[12] Here we are treated to one of C.H.'s most egregious "exaggerations." He most certainly used the ferry boats and the Sacramento River steamers simply because our family owned them! And he went by ship to Seattle and Juneau to seal a trade deal for his father-in-law, Hyrum Milton. In 1872 he went to Europe with his family, sailing on the *Empress of Russia* by way of Macao, Singapore, and Cape Town. On the very same run two years later the vessel was destroyed in a typhoon off of Manila with a heavy loss of life.

[13] Built by Wm. Jones & Sons in the Brooklyn Yards in 1848. The voyage we made was the ship's second trip to California. She had a long, narrow hull and tall masts that carried tremendous clouds of canvas — the clipper ship was built for speed, and the *Tronka* could do 18 knots. She made the San Francisco run in 100 days averaging $6\frac{1}{4}$ knots. The gold rush spurred development of the clipper ships. People wanted a "fast" passage to California, but, more important, they wanted a means of bringing along substantial personal freight: tools, machinery, books, merchandise, etc., at reasonable freight rates. This could not be done by overland transport, and the transcontinental railroads were decades away.

[14] Surely C.H. knew that the name Yerba Buena had been officially changed to San Francisco some months before.

to the sun, to test my sinews in mortal combat.[15]

Land! Earth! I scooped up a handful of San Francisco mud[16] and pressed it to my face—a baptism! From that day to this—63 years—I swear I am not French or Italian or English or New English or American: I am a Californian. My eyes are set westward to the setting sun. I was one of 25,000 emigrants to come to California in 1849. My soul was born on the Pacific slope.

I feel a deeper kinship with a Chinese herb doctor than I do with a blue-eyed Dane or an Englishman, because the Celestial[17] and I are Pacific kin. Sea water is life's first blood. I have seen this green and golden land fill with all manner of men and women, and I love them because they turned their backs on home and friends and family to let their sweat irrigate a new pasture.

On that very first hour in San Francisco, the stentorian cries of the leather-lunged hotel and boarding house drummers in my ears, I set a course through the shanties of the Chinese,[18] seeking higher ground.

---

[15] C.H. had just turned 20. He was an even six-foot tall, 180 pounds, and very muscular by virtue of the manual labor he did independently of what piddling duties he did for John-Cowe by way of his parents. From age 12 C.H. was a for-hire stable mucker. "The secret of success," he often expounded, "is never to work for wages. Work by the job. A man wants you to muck-out five stables. You give him a price—say $25. Agreed! Shake hands. You go to the commons and find five lads in need of cash. You hire them at $4 a stable. Let's see. How much do you make on that deal, Bayard?"

[16] C.H. is back on track.

[17] China was known as the Celestial Kingdom, hence the name for the individual.

[18] Another C.H. fiction. Up to 1850 a mere handful of Chinese had come to California. Chum Ming, who arrived in 1848, was the first. He got word back to a friend in Canton, Cheong Yum, that there was gold in the mountains of this new country. Ship masters in Hong Kong and Canton circulated glowing reports and flaming advertisements on the wonders of California. San Francisco was singled out as "The Market of the Three Barbarian Tribes." In 1850 40 vessels sailed to California from Hong Kong. By year's end in 1851, 25,000 Chinese had come to California. At

Here was my first venture into the strangeness of red streamers, the feel of sandalwood and the sweet smell of jasmine: dingy buildings that were home and fan-tan parlor; home and chop house; home and grocery store; home and laundry. Their inhabitants wore quilted jackets and full blue cotton breeches reaching to the knees. The soles on their sandals were an inch thick. Under the black beehive caps hung sacred pigtails.

Without bothering to wash the soil of California from my mouth, I pointed to and subsequently downed a bowl of white rice. Happy to be alive, happy to be 20 years old, happy to be on land, I pointed again and downed a second bowl of white rice. Then I tried to strike up a conversation with the first Californian with whom I had the pleasure of dining. But, alas, there was no opportunity to discuss anything more esoteric than white rice. Pity. I attended a coloquy at Harvard Divinity School in which a Harvard professor stated Emerson and the Transcendentalists were not to be dismissed lightly, that their exploration of Eastern Religion was more than a protest against the lack of spirituality in the mainstream Western religions.[19]

From the chop house I walked up a steep path to where I could see a wide plaza topped by a flagpole displaying the stars and bars. I paused often to gaze over the retreating bay—a forest of masts tracing lazy circles in the salt air—a body of water so vast the distant east shore was a line of haze.

---

first the Chinese were considered a novelty, but as their numbers swelled in the gold diggings they were viewed as competition—serious competition to be harshly dealt with by the "Americans" who had won California fair and square in a war with Mexico.

[19] There is one subject I never brought up with my grandfather, nor did I inquire into it with my parents: C.H. was in Boston in his late teens. Why did he not make an effort to attend Harvard? The Harvard professor was Theodore Price. In his later years he recanted his criticism of the Transcendentalists and became a Zen Buddist. He is remembered for the lines: "I will walk with fate / And thus compel the Jade to go my way./ A jackal falling down a well said / 'Here I camp today.'"

Here were anchored vessels flying the flags of England, France, Spain, Portugal, New Granada, Russia, Peru, Tahiti, Genoa, Bremen...and, of course, the United States....

The Parker House dominated the plaza. Across the way stood the City Hotel, a bright yellow and red board advertising its rates: $25 per week; $20 more for meals. Porters ran in and out of both hotels, toting luggage recently removed from the now idle fleet in the bay.

This was Portsmouth Square, the very heart of this young city.[20] I sat down on an abandoned crate and let the sounds and sights of a new world come to me. Here was humanity in perpetual motion: oval-faced Lascars, small-eyed Kanackers, zarape-clad Mexicans, Chileans, Peruvians, flannel-shirted Saxons, Negroes, Feejians, tattooed New Zealanders, Chinese, jet-black Abyssinians, fiery-eyed Malays, turbaned Turks, Russians....[21]

Of women there were few. Likewise the elderly.[22]

"The latest news from the States!" cried a voice I immediately recognized. It was Mr. Laney, a fellow-passenger on the *Tronka*.

Merchants, idlers, gold-seekers, and scholars perked an ear toward Mr. Laney—then they became a mob rushing to buy one of his 90-day-old newspapers. As part of Lord John-Cowe's 20-pieces-of luggage entourage aboard the *Tronka* I had been snobbishly bemused by Mr. Laney's meager shipboard possessions. He lived out of one small portmanteau, but continually hovered over two cartons crammed full of these New York newspapers. Mr. Laney

---

[20] The name honors Commodore John D. Sloat's *U.S.S. Portsmouth* which entered San Francisco Bay on July 9, 1846, and seized Alta California for the United States.

[21] C.H. "borrows" this catalog from the *Journal* of William Perkins, a Sonora merchant.

[22] On October 21, 1849, Nathan Spear died of heart disease. He was 47 years of age—one of the oldest inhabitants of San Francisco. Spear was a partner of Jacob P. Leese, who formed the first mercantile establishment in San Francisco.

afforded us a snitch of relief from the agony of the sea. When we came face to face with the dreadful Horn, Mr. Laney led our shrieking lamentations: we for our lives, he for his newspapers.

In fact, the jokes directed at Mr. Laney and the *New York Herald* became so gross the captain, finally, ordered the subject off limits at the mess, fearing, I supposed at the time, that his absolute authority would be eroded by the incessant talk on so tiny a target.

Mr. Laney, I felt, was crazy.

After half-an-hour watching Mr. Laney sell 600 two-cent 90-day-old newspapers for a dollar per each, I knew which of us stood nearest to ignorance.

Even then I correctly sensed that money was the key to freedom. The love of money might be the root of evil, but money itself is a most blissful friend, to be spoken of in the same reverence one reserves for an old wife or a faithful dog.

When Mr. Laney[23] concluded his business, he ambled over to where I stood probably mouth agape. A lesser person would have sunk his teeth into my flesh, seeking the terrene taste of vindication, and saying, perhaps, "Can I interest you in a 90-day-old newspaper—provided your master has given you your weekly dollar required for its purchase?"

Instead, this excellent man said: "Ah, Caesar (pronouncing it correctly: CHE-sar-eh), you're looking better. I really worried about you out there."

"Thank you, Mr. Laney," I answered. "I'm feeling much better, but I'm puzzled: how did you get your newspapers up here so quickly? I don't think the *Tronka* has tied-up yet."

"Gold is the picklock that never fails," he answered. "The ship's crew is amenable to bribery so I fixed it with them to have my papers and myself delivered to shore even before the sun rose this morning. The crew, incidentally, is at this

---

[23] Born Charles Robert Laney in Brooklyn, New York, he was listed in the San Francisco city registry every year through 1857. He drowned off the Farallon Islands when the bark *Hunter* went aground.

moment jumping ship and leaving your fellow passengers to make their own off-loading rituals."

This was disquieting news. This means John-Cowe would need my muscle-power to help with luggage (he had round-the-clock possession of the silver dollars).

Mr. Laney knew what was going through my mind. "First," he said, "let us repair to a grog shop for two 90-day-old East Coast newspapers worth of a welcome home drink."

"Welcome home?" I asked.

"Young man," he said, "you are young and strong and uncommonly smart. You are California's bridegroom."

"Bridegroom?" I asked. "What does that mean?"

"It means," my friend said, "you will marry this place and live your entire life and die here."

"But," he added, "let us find a liquor bar if such an establishment exists in San Francisco."

Mr. Laney making jokes! Every other business establishment sold alcohol, by the barrel, gallon, quart, pint, glass, or shot. As it was, fate led us into the darkened interior of a place bearing the uncommon name, "Nellie's Fleas"[24] — a circumstance upon which my destiny pirouetted.

I recall, as we passed out of the sunlight into the liquor bar, having had a twinge of conscience: I had already over-extended my morning jaunt.

My parents would be expecting me to help make the ship-to-shore transfer, and John-Cowe would certainly leave all the work to them. I covered my guilt with the knowledge that my parents were resourceful. If Mr. Laney could get an entire ship's crew to do a rather minor service for him, I felt my parents would manage.

Liberty is given by nature even to mute animals, and I was

---

[24] Nell Fulton ran a bawdy house in Sydney, Australia, during a time when the locals were plagued by an infestation of fleas. Nell, who basked in the reputation of her "clean" girls, offered a free go at the merchandise if anyone found a flea on one of the girls. The promotion ended when some customers figured out fleas were transportable.

enjoying the banquet of freedom that was mine by simply sitting down to it.

Nellie's Fleas was comfortably filled with men of every description and persuasion in need of an early morning "eye opener." We were interrupted by the appearance at the open door of a crew of roughnecks muscling in a magnificent oak panel complete with several rows of beveled mirrors.

I knew this panel! It held a conspicuous place in the *Tronka*'s hold, and now it was going to be the backbar in the very first liquor saloon I had ever entered.

It seemed every one of the men in that saloon took a hand in aligning and anchoring the panel to the back wall. When it was secure, Mike O'Farrell, the burly Australian, his left eye gone, co-owner of Nellie's Fleas, declared: "Drinks on the house." Pandemonium. Cheers. Whistles. Until Mike's brother and partner, Robby, stood on a chair, got silence, and said: "Limit of two drinks except the crew that fetched it from the ship — six drinks."

Mr. Laney talked about his life in New York. He had been a back-bench accountant. He told of his wife and seven (this fact amazed me!) children, and how he would be able to send for them — not, I thought, on his newspaper venture earnings. If he had an ace up his sleeve he did not say nor did I inquire.

Hypocrites weep, and you cannot tell their tears apart from a saint's; but no bad man ever laughed sweetly. Mr. Laney's laugh was pure sweetness, and I knew that the crew and passengers — me especially included — aboard the *Tronka* had done an injustice to this sweet man.

Our shots before us, I studied how the others handled the whiskey and I did the same, turning my back to the bar, throwing my head back, opening my mouth to receive the shot. When I opened my eyes I received the shock of my young life — not from the liquor because strong drink was no stranger in the surroundings of my former life: a heroic-size painting on the wall I was now facing for the first time — a nude — lying on a satin bed — a nude with legs wide apart—my first view, albeit a fairly competent artist's rendition, of that divine orifice that rules and often ruins every male on earth, from Adam onward.

Innocence and mystery never dwell long together.[25]

Most artists, I learned later in life, treat nudity with some reverence. I'm sure the oil on my nude was still wet, and that the artist[26] was off somewhere seeking inspiration for his next masterpiece. In any event, my nude was clean-shaven, so to speak, and printed in handsome letters on that pink curve of her Mound of Venus was the legend *Edepol nunc nos tempus est malas peioris fieri*.

"Do you know Latin?" Mr. Laney asked.

"Afraid not," I answered. It was not the mystery of the Latin that held my full attention, and I'm sure my riveted amazement was much easier to read than the Latin legend.

Mr. Laney spoke: "How old are you, Caesar?"

"Twenty, last month," I said.

"Close your mouth," he said. Then he patted me on my arm and quietly slipped out of the barroom.

Mike O'Farrell looked me over with his one good eye. "Know what it says?" he asked, referring to the Latin.

"No idea," I answered.

At this time I had been on dry land in a city I had only heard about previously for less than two hours, when in walks a second person I had known on the *Tronka*.

Billy Tremaine.[27] A deckhand completing his first voyage. A devil-may-care sort, younger than me by two years, who displayed uncommon courage when it came to climbing up to the crow's nest in the worst of horrible weather while all I could do is lie on my back on the deck praying for death.

---

[25] A quote from Madame Necker. I have no idea what it means.

[26] Joseph Hendrix by name, a teacher of Latin in a former life. His paintings—complete with Latin footnotes—were scattered about San Francisco. Many were of the same girl, but none other that I was aware of, in the same pose.

[27] Billy Tremaine figures prominently in C.H.'s "curious enterprise."

Most of the other sailors had spared no *sotte voce* comments on my seamanship, but Billy Tremaine had done worse: he had ignored me.

"Hello, Bill," I said, extending my hand.

"Hello," he said. His handshake was firm. No matter what our stations might have been aboard ship, here we met as fellow pioneers in a brave, new world.[28]

"I've been studying my Latin," I said by way of starting a conversation. I pointed to the nude.

"What's it say?" Billy asked.

Mike O"Farrell, busy pouring drinks for the backbar celebrants, caught Billy's question. "What do you think it says?" he asked.

"Something to do with quim," answered Billy.

"Holy name!" cried Mike. "We have a bloody genius come belly-up to my bar." He scanned the room with his one good eye and it fell on a gray-haired ancient boozer.[29] "Parker," he cried, "These youngsters need a Latin lesson. Bring your glass!"

Parker's glass, of course, was empty. He held it up to be filled, turned to the nude and waited for the room to quiet down. When he had the audience's attention, he recited, first in Latin then in English in a timbre-dripping stage voice: "The immortal words of the Roman playwright Titus Maccius Platus. I quote—*Edepol nunc nos tempus est malas peioris fieri*—in English—Now's the time for bad girls to become worse still."

Billy Tremaine, it turns out, had kin in Monterey. He had no plans to get back on the *Tronka* except to fetch his pay and his gear. There would be no problem because he had signed up for a one-way trip. If the truth be told, the *Tronka* would

---

[28] C.H. always displayed a penchant for quoting Shakespeare. This reference to "a brave, new world" is doubly apt because it comes from *The Tempest*—the very condition the two men had experienced.
[29] He could not have been too ancient. The most elderly citizen in this city of young men at the time was but 55 years of age.

not find crew enough to put to sea for several months for Billy Tremaine's mates may have been able to weather the Horn, but they could not cure gold fever. Most of the 600 ships at anchor in the bay would be abandoned.

Looking back at the far away morning, the fates had me in mind for just as Parker was receiving the last pat on the back for a Latin job well done, into Nellie's Fleas came the *Tronka*'s second mate, Martin Bledsoe — my third shipmate.

Bledsoe was as mean as he was ugly. It was he who disciplined the crew. He often recalled with a sneering degree of joy the "gone years" when flogging was the standard and not the exception. He walked up to us and without so much as a greeting said, "Billy, get back on the ship and get your pay." To me he said, "Get your ass back to the ship. You're wanted by John-Cowe to do your work." To Mike O'Farrell: "No more of your rotten liquor to this fine Christian gentleman," meaning me, delivered with dripping sarcasm.

Billy scampered out of Nellie's Fleas. One-eyed Mike reached under the bar and snarled at Bledsoe: "Unless you want your scalp blessed with a second harelip, I suggest you turn around..." Mike and Bledsoe at the same instant at this point in Mike's warning slammed down on the bar identical heavy wooden boat cleats, the weapon *de jour*.

They stood amazed — then Mike started laughing and Bledsoe stood back. It was a startling development — a perfectly timed *pas de deux*.

So startled by the simultaneous bangs, I too laughed.

Not able to handle Mike and a barroom full of his friends, Bledsoe turned to me. "I'd like to crack your head," he said, glaring into my eyes.

Mike intervened. "You know this man?" he asked Bledsoe.

"He's not a man," said the second mate, "he's a pasty-faced half-cock servant of some British lord." He dangled the boat cleat under my nose. "No doubt amuses his master by taking the likes of this up his arse."

I should not have done what I ended up doing; but Bledsoe left me with no choice. I should have counted to 10, but I had no choice. I should have counted to 20, but I had no choice. I blame my first two hours in California, Mr. Laney making $600 in a half-hour. I blame the nude. I blame the utter joy of standing on firm ground.

I had all the time in the world to think this out. Like the audience waiting to have Parker deliver the line from Titus Maccius Platus, the audience held its breath.

Thanks to Bledsoe I had come early to this vital crossroads in my life: freedom or servitude. The wrong choice would haunt me until my last breath.

I doubled up my fist until the sinews cried for relief, and hit the second mate square on the nose. Fortune is always on the side of the largest battalions—but more important, she smiles on the army that delivers the first blow.

I felt cartilage crumbling. Bledsoe, probably more surprised than hurt, lurched forward. He raised the wooden boat cleat. The debate was over. I remember thinking: "He wants to kill me." Immediately followed by: "I want to kill him." And as this colloquy was reaching its climax, Mike wrenched the boat cleat out of Bledsoe's hand, leaving his nose open to a decisive second attack. I struck. Bledsoe stumbled backward and sat down on the floor. I hit him square upon his crown with a brass spittoon, then poured the spent offerings of a hundred brown cuds over his bleeding and broken head.

Nellie's Fleas exploded. Mike was over the plank in one hurdle. He grabbed half of me while a squad of his devotees took hold of the other half and out into the street I was thrown.

San Francisco weather! I remember thinking: What happened to the sunshine? Where did all this fog come from? I also remember in that instance of departure a visual mixture of Bledsoe's smashed nose, wild faces, animated beards, the rich black walnut backbar, and the nude.[30]

I landed in the middle of the busy street at John-Cowe's feet. Following Bledsoe's humiliating pronouncement to a bar-full of probable degenerates, the last person I wanted or expected to see was my parents' employer.

"Caesar," he said, "you are wanted to help your parents with my things."

Looking back, there are many things I wish I had said in response, but my favorite is: "This is California. Get your own damned things." Alas, I did not say anything. I reached behind me, gathered up a fresh horse turd and hurled it in John-Cowe's direction.

A fresh horse turd was my Declaration of Independence![31]

We stood facing one another when a freight wagon turned a corner, the driver shouting, "'Round the corner, Sally!" separated us.

When the wagon passed John-Cowe was gone and with him my strings to the past. Thus it was that I became a free citizen of the Pacific Basin. I had vanquished Bledsoe and his

---

[30] When Nellie's Fleas was closed by the revived San Francisco Committee of Vigilance in 1856, the black walnut backbar was sold at auction to an interior designer. C.H. ran across it in the bathroom of a Nob Hill banker while attending a reception honoring patrons of the local opera. His first inclination was to inject a bit of spice into the dull soirée by giving the true and unvarnished history of that wooden slab, including a history of Nellie and some choice passages in Latin, but he knew Nana Burgundia would not be pleased. [Note: In response to escalating crime, San Francisco merchants first organized a Committee of Vigilance in 1851. On June 9 John Jenkins of Sydney, Australia, was hanged for stealing a safe from a business. At that time in California, grand larceny was punishable by death. These irregular militias hanged seven others, deported several Sydneyites, and forced several elected officials to resign.]

[31] This is undoubtedly fiction. Ours is the kind of family in which family episodes are retold almost ritualistically (certain occasions demand certain stories be retold). Never had I heard this story until I read C.H.'s journal. So far as I know, his split from John-Cowe's retinue was amicable. C.H.'s parents likewise understood that once in California he would strike out on his own.

scurrilous libel, said my good-bye to my Parents' employer, had a first look at the gates of paradise, had two shots of whiskey under my belt, and $31[32] in my pocket.

It was my desire to put distance between me and Nellie's Fleas. For all I knew, the brass spittoon may have killed Bledsoe. At least, if not dead, he would be mightily vexed. A mile north of Portsmouth Square, I rented two blankets, a rough table, a looking glass, a wash basin, a three-legged chair, and a cot—$25 for the week, in advance—another $15 if I wanted breakfast and dinner, which I did not having already mastered the art of ordering food in a Chinese chop shop. The hostelry's dirt floor reassured me that it would not require me to sweep it.

At high noon I fell upon said cot and enjoyed a most delicious sleep.

---

[32] The truth is C.H. had well over $500 on his person when he made landfall in San Francisco, and a credit secured by hard cash of $1500 with the Farmers and Merchants Trust of Boston. In addition to his stable mucking, he dried herbs and sold them door-to-door. He had both rosemary and lavender hair treatments, and dried thyme to spice up traditional clam chowder.

2

Judge Milton's Court

I spent the first two weeks in San Francisco hiding out from my father, who I knew would be hounded into action by my mother. Bledsoe had lived and he swore out a complaint against me, served to my parents and John-Cowe and one-eyed Mike O'Farrell.

My mother's only comment was, "If my boy hit you on the head with a brass spittoon you deserved it. Now go away."

My father conducted a low intensity search. He visited the grog shops, chop houses and other places of amusement with, of course, no luck.[33] He even went to the bull and bear pavilion after mass supposedly looking for me but actually to witness this cruel sport.[34]

I divided my time between the San Francisco branch of the Sons of Temperance, and the court of Hyrum Milton.[35] My evening meal I usually took at the Bay Side where clams, mussels, sea urchin and limpets were plentiful and

---

[33] As stated previously (footnote 31) C.H. was always in touch with his parents after arriving in San Francisco.

[34] Bull and bear baiting, in which trained dogs attacked tethered bulls or bears, was a favorite recreation of Queen Elizabeth. The California version of this bloodsport pitted bull against bear. Usually the bull attacked and the bear fought a defensive battle—hence the stock market terms "Bull Market" for an advancing market; and "Bear Market" for a retreating market. In early Spanish days in California, grizzlies were plentiful, especially where livestock was slaughtered and butchered. Horsemen would lasso bears and run them down the pueblo streets.

[35] Of all of C.H.'s fiction, this is the most egregious. Milton was never a judge. In fact, the descriptions of his court which follow are taken almost verbatim from the *Annals of San Francisco and History of California* by

cheap — but few oysters, which my Boston palate craved. This is an enigma, for today the Pacific oyster is plentiful.

Judge Milton, as you shall see, became a major influence of my life. He was a Massachusetts Brahmin who had been in San Francisco with his family[36] for more than a year, making him a "town father," a ranking equal to that lofty height enjoyed by the Mission padres. He was a competent lawyer;[37] a gourmet; a virtuoso on the mandolin; a patron of the theater;[38] and he spent his Sundays not in church, but botanizing in the surrounding hills. He was, in short, a Renaissance Man.

Milton had been authorized to open and hold a court of the First Instance, with civil jurisdiction only, and in cases involving sums exceeding $100.

His honor had a sovereign contempt for Buncombe speeches, legal technicalities, learned opinions, and triumphantly-cited precedence.

He sat on a rickety chair, his feet perched higher than his head upon a small mantel over the fireplace, in which a few damp sticks of wood were keeping each other warm by the aid of a very limited supply of burning coals.

His honor employed himself in paring his corns or scraping his nails, while the "learned counsel" briefly

---

Frank Soule, John Gihon, and James Nisbet. "Annals" entries are quoted throughout C.H.'s work. On December 12, 1849, the government authorized William B. Almond to open and hold a court of the First Instance. It is Almond and his courtroom antics which C.H. describes here. I have no explanation as to why he wanted us to believe Milton was this person. Indeed, he leaves it to us to resolve how Milton could be judge and lawyer, both at once.

[36] A rarity. Hyrum and his wife, Mary Lawrence Milton, and their three daughters — all named after wine varieties: Champagnes ("Agnes"), Zinfandella ("Della"), and Burgundia — by themselves doubled the number of eligible marriageable American women in California.

[37] We have dealt with this "fact."

[38] It was Milton who brought Lola Montez to San Francisco; and it was Milton who was the first to recognize Lotta Crabtree's talents. Lola and Lotta were neighbors in Grass Valley during one brief period.

presented his case, and called the first witness, whom the judge personally instructed without changing his position, to tell all he knew about the matter at hand.

The witness is no sooner done, when the counsel calls another—but Judge Milton informs him that it is unnecessary to pursue the matter further—the judge has made up his mind!

The lawyer is flabbergasted. "You will at least hear us speak to the point of law?" he fairly screams.

"That would be a great waste of time," Judge Milton answers, "and time is very precious." With this he hands down his judgment.

Young lawyers were not pleased with Hyrum's summary method of disposing justice. To these the opportunity to make a speech so they could hear with pleasure their oratory prowess, the purpose of which was to render a clear case obscure, though it doubtless serves to display the extent of their wisdom and intelligence. This to attorneys was as consequential as meat and drink to a starving man. These attorneys simply could not live without such attention.

During the week that I hid out in Judge Milton's courtroom, I saw him bested but once. He had decided against a young attorney and his client in less than two minutes. Down came the gavel, but the attorney picked up a book and began reading from it aloud.

Judge Milton reminded the young man that judgment had been rendered, and all further remarks useless.

"I am aware of that," said the attorney, "but I thought I would simply read a passage or two to convince you what an old fool Blackstone was."

I was the only person in the room who did not laugh. Indeed, Milton laughed the loudest. I did not know who Blackstone was.

The bulk of Milton's court business had to do with settling claims against owners and masters of ships brought by passengers and, more rarely, by crew. The law of the sea wherein the ship captain was absolute took historic precedence over land law. Milton's decisions were generally against the defendants—the party most likely to have the ready cash to pay court costs.

But, this is harsh judgment on Milton's integrity. The simple fact is that during the great rush of emigrants to California, the most shameful impositions—moldy food, crowded quarters, brim-full chamber pots spilling over—were thrust upon passengers. Once in the open sea the ship's captain was absolute sovereign and the last thing he held in his imagination was that in rude, unsettled California there would be a court of law whose edicts were backed by the port authorities backed, in turn, by the United States Navy.

After the morning court sessions I would take the back streets to the Temperance House where I read what they called their "side literature." The woman in charge—a rather pleasant, friendly sort, perhaps this side of 50—took me under her wing. Her conversation consisted of two compartments. The first had to do with the fact she had never tasted liquor and consequently would soon be in heaven drinking something called "Adam's Ale." Her second subject was her recently deceased husband. If he was half as good a man as she painted him to be, he no doubt was assigned to replace St. Peter as heaven's greeter. Whenever she presented her dead husband's litany, she would reach over and lay her hand on my forearm.

While women have fewer vices than men, they have stronger prejudices.[39] Mabel Clark (that is not her name nor did this episode in my life occur at the Temperance House) was fervently prejudiced against strong drink—and, of course, her husband was not a saint but a fall-down drunk.

All this was revealed at our fourth meeting.

"Did he abuse you?" I asked.

"Worse," she said. And now her hand gripped my arm.

---

[39] A quote from Dr. J. V. C. Smith.

"He ignored me."

We ended up in the basement. She would not let me see let alone examine the treasure on view to the whole world at Nellie's Fleas. I tried to kiss her, but she demurred. She gathered up her dress, waited for me to drop my pants, took a step closer, shut her eyes, and guided me home. We did it standing up. She did her best to stifle her moans and pretty much succeeded. My first time standing up!

I went no more to the Temperance House. Instead I spent a great deal more time over my late afternoon meal at the Bay Side where I became acquainted with the cook-proprietor, Luigi Crespi, a citizen of Genoa and, he claimed, a distant cousin of Christopher Columbus.

The Genoese, he pointed out, were shrewd traders—known as the "Jews of the Mediterranean." He ended up in San Francisco, practically destitute, because a fellow Genoese "out-shrewded"[40] him. Luigi regaled me with seafood and improbable Genoese folklore. Trying to explain just how frugal his people were, he declared, "It is the Genoese who crucified Christ and I know how we can tell. One of them told the Savoir to cross his feet so they could save a nail."

"Sacrilegious but funny," a voice behind me said—a voice I immediately recognized. It came from the Honorable Judge Hyrum Milton. With him, age 17, was his daughter Burgundia, the most beautiful girl I had ever seen. Milton was immaculately dressed, even to a beaver hat, striped trousers and powder-blue waistcoat. Obviously he was not going to his court room where he always appeared in merchant's gear. The girl was in a rose-colored frock—suitable for any type formal outing.

"Caesar," he said...how in hell did he know my name? We had never spoken!!! "I'd like you to meet my daughter, Burgundia." Then to the girl: "You know Mr. Crespi." Luigi

---

[40] I suppose such a word exists.

Crespi bowed, and beamed. "Caesar Honore is the young man I was telling you about," continued Milton.

I was stunned. And silent.

Milton made mention of their dress by passing a hand over their opulent clothes, adding by way of explanation, "We're going to hear the French singer."[41]

Obviously Milton had one of his assistants do some checking up on me. And obviously, when he had all the facts, Milton performed one of his famous two-minute judgment routines, and I had passed — passed what? And why?

I did not have long to wait for the denouement.

Hyrum waited for Luigi to return to his kitchen, then he motioned for me to join him at the far end of the room where we would be out of earshot of the four or five diners busy with their food.

"I hadn't seen you in court the past few days, and fearing you had left my jurisdiction I took the chance of finding you here," he said.

"But...." is all I could say.

Burgundia threw back her head and laughed. "He can talk!" she said.

Her father smiled, but bade her be quiet with a hand gesture.

"I received a bench warrant for your arrest initiated by one Martin Bledsoe, an officer aboard the *Tronka*," Milton said. "Attempted murder, the weapon being a brass spittoon.

"Now, I know this Bledsoe character and I was curious to know who had finally stood up to him, albeit with a brass spittoon."

Burgundia spoke up, "Daddy has a job for you."

"What sort of job?" I asked.

Hyrum grabbed the floor: "Please, Burgundia, let's not be distracted with any more of your earth-shaking observations...

---

[41] Mme. Claudia Fentralle, who toured America from East Coast to West and then retired on her earnings.

'he can talk!' "

She sat back and indicated she would be "a good girl," but she kept a steady, bemused gaze straight into my eyes and soul.

"I am certain the spittoon incident was warranted. Mike O'Farrell, a respectable businessman whose only shortcoming is having poor taste when it comes to art, gave the court his sworn affidavit that the spittoon was justified.

"I discussed my proposal with your parents...."

"My parents?" What was going on!

"Fine people," said the judge. "Incidentally, they'd like to see you now that you're no longer a murderer-on-the-run. They're at the City Hotel on Portsmouth Square."

Burgundia giggled: "Across the square from Nellie's Fleas."

Here was my opportunity to show off. I knew a bit of Latin: "The *locus facinus*."

"The what?" Burgundia asked.

"The scene of the crime," her father said.

All very amusing and all very mysterious. What, exactly, was going on? How were my parents involved? Why was it necessary to talk to them without first talking to me? Was this "job" "Daddy" has for me legal? Does it involve anything to do with a voyage?

The judge read my mind. "Despite squashing Bledsoe's action," he said, "you have a disturbing-the-peace charge against you plus a possible action by Mike O'Farrell for the destruction of a brass spittoon—all very minor stuff—but the problem is you fled the scene and for a month you were a fugitive...."

"I was in your court room!" I cried. "How in hell does that make me a fugitive?"

Judge Milton appeared delighted by my response. "Better than I had hoped," he said to Burgundia. To me he said, "Come to our home tomorrow evening for dinner. Anyone can direct you. You will be apprised of the particulars of your fine for disturbing the peace and fleeing my jurisdiction. The spittoon thing you'll have to take up with O'Farrell — that is, when you return to San Francisco. I would appreciate you not frequenting Nellie's Fleas. And better not go to the Temperance House.

"Meanwhile, go see your parents. They are fine people."

The Temperance House! Does he know everything about me — does she know? I can best describe my state of mind at that moment as dazed — beyond dazed.

My parents welcomed me back into the fold. Lord John-Cowe was absent, thankfully, but I sensed something fundamentally different in the dynamics between that gentleman and my parents. I based this not on anything said, but rather on what was not said. Strangely, I thought at that time that Hyrum Milton's visit was responsible for this sea-change.[42]

"Dinner" in California means seven p.m. Strict punctuality is a cheap virtue.[43] I was at the Milton home at the appointed hour, more eager to see the golden-haired girl who lived here than to learn of my fate at the hands of Hyrum Milton.

Burgundia opened the door and greeted me with, "You've changed your clothes."

I was primed to keep up with her and had mentally rehearsed my retorts to all possible subjects she might bring up — from the weather (foggy) to Nellie's Fleas (Mr. Laney's

---

[42] Hyrum Milton indeed! There had been not one meeting between the "judge" and C.H.'s parents but several — and these were not casual social visits or meetings to inquire into C.H.'s character, but business negotiations. Milton needed a couple to take over a room and board establishment he suddenly acquired and Enrico and Carolina Honore, with years of experience catering to the privileged, seemed an ideal fit. Besides, this was California — the land of opportunity and self-reliance. This arrangement between my great-grandparents and my future great-grandfather proved prosperous for the Honore-Milton clan.

[43] Here we have a rare steal from Ben Franklin.

newspaper bonanza / invited in for a drink to celebrate) to—heaven forbid—the Temperance House...but I was not prepared to respond to her opening gambit.

No need. The mother of the house smiled a warm greeting.

"Mother," said the daughter, "this is Caesar Honore."

"Ah," said Mary Lawrence Milton, the well-spring of Burgundia's beauty, "The young man who is going to go to Monterey for Daddy."

Monterey! Will everyone on earth know about this "job" before I do?

The dinner, served on chinaware,[44] was notable in that I made the acquaintance of the Milton middle daughter, Zinfandella ("Della").[45] The third and eldest daughter, Champagnes (Agnes) was married to a young physician about to make his mark in San Francisco, or so Burgundia assured me. During the course of the evening I found it rather refreshing that the four Miltons only spoke well of one-another and, for that matter, of anyone or any thing.

---

[44] Various plates, saucers and platters from the Miltons' San Francisco china have come down through the family generations. These items are an undecorated smooth white—so superior it is known as "artificial jade."

[45] The Miltons named all three of their daughters after wine varieties.

Zinfandel, also known as Primitivo, is a black-skinned wine grape introduced in the "heel" of Italy in the 18th Century. The infant Zinfandella was born with a full head of jet-black hair. Della, still living at home, was at this time betrothed to John Decarli who ran some sort of family business in North Carolina. They never married. When Della finally gave up on John she joined the Sisters the Presentation, a cloistered Catholic order which founded a San Francisco branch on November 13, 1854. She ended up in Fargo, North Dakota. Upon joining the order and taking her final vows, she had to commit to seeing her family but one time—at the funeral of the first of her parents to die. This happened in 1863 when Milton died.

Champagnes ("Agnes") as the first born received the name of the "miracle" wine associated with royalty.

Burgundia was more a political statement than a direct reference to a variety of grape. Milton liked the fact that the inheritance laws of the Napoleonic Code decreed that vineyards in Burgundy (actually, in all of France) must be split equally among one's heirs. That appealed to Milton's sense of fair play.

The dinner over, and now — at long last — to business. Della left the table to help the maid-cook with the clean-up, but Mary and Burgundia remained sitting where they were, prepared to weigh in.

Mary did more than "weigh in." She unleashed a crash of thunder. "Hyrum, through some business dealings that none of us understands, has come to own a whore house in Monterey," she said, "and we want you to move it to Sonora in the gold country."

Hyrum added: "We need someone like you, an unknown to the city with obvious skills...."

Burgundia interjected: "With a spittoon...."

Milton smiled at the *ad lib*, then continued: "...with no known big-mouthed acquaintances who would spread it around San Francisco that Hyrum Milton, possible senator[46] from California, runs a bawdy house."

I was flabbergasted. I hardly knew what to say, so I said: "What makes you think I wouldn't talk it about?" I knew the answer and if they tried to wiggle out of it, I was prepared to walk out the door.

Hyrum chose his words carefully: "Your parents. I am sincere in saying I found them to be fine people, and I knew their son would likewise be meritorious...."

I spoke: "And if for any reason I ruined your chance of becoming a senator, the financial support you so generously offered to my parents would be withdrawn. Is that not the case?"

Mary: "That is exactly the case."

Me: "Blackmail."

Hyrum: "Insurance."

Me: "I appreciate your honesty. You will not regret any business venture you enter into with my parents." Burgundia, sitting next to me, laid a hand on my arm — the second female to do so within the past week. The gesture startled me into

[46] The honor of being California's first U. S. Senators would go to John C. Fremont, the "Pathfinder," and William Gwin.

remembering Mabel Clark and the baseness of that encounter compared to the uplifting innocent nobility of this encounter of the flesh.

Mary: "Then you accept?"

Me: "We haven't touched on compensation."

Hyrum: "Because you are not putting any capital in this venture...."

Me, interrupting: "No capital! My youth is my capital. My loyalty to my employer is my capital."

Hyrum, continuing: "Wagons have to be purchased, horses have to be fed, nails and hammers and saws have to be purchased, workers have to be paid and fed...."

Burgundia, interrupting: "Unless you are going to do all the work yourself...."

Hyrum, continuing: "...then there is the matter of the care and feeding of the girls...."

Me: "WHAT GIRLS???"

Mary: "I prefer they are put down in the books as 'merchandise'."

Burgundia: "They would probably prefer that, too."

Hyrum: "All in all, I'm going to be 12-15 thousand dollars out of pocket. We should have the Vista del Mar up and operating in Sonora in three or four months. Then we sell it and we split the net profit four ways—one-quarter for you and one-quarter for each of my three girls."

Me: "Why go to all the trouble of hauling a building across California? Why not just cut down some Sonora trees and build your own whorehouse?"

Hyrum: "Good lumber is so expensive ship masters are finding it profitable to sail to China and haul back disassembled frames and prepared walls for what is known here as 'China Houses.' The man I acquired the Vista del Mar from erected a great Chinese palace...."

Mary: "It's beautiful—all hand-sanded and red-lacquered panels, all fitted together like a great Chinese puzzle box."

There were more details which need no recounting here. I was satisfied with the deal, especially as it related to my parents and the opportunity this gave them to corner a bit of security in their declining years.[47]

I spent several days at the Milton home preparing for this "curious enterprise" as Della christened it. There was a great deal of paperwork involved, setting up lines of credit, letters of introduction, updating the impressive passbooks of the seven young ladies.[48] Hyrum pointed out that the Vista Del Mar, was not just a whorehouse, but a "happy whorehouse," thanks entirely to the seven young ladies who ran the business without benefit of a madam (although Rick Brazelton—more on him later—was always on the premises, out of sight, should the girls need help). Their leader was 23-year-old Dandelion (the bank accepted this as a legitimate given name) Ralston, who had managed to save $16,323 at $2 a throw. The other six young ladies had savings ranging from $5000 to $10,000. The Del Mar/Monte Seven did not share Milton's faith in banks and as soon as he was no longer in the whorehouse picture, they withdrew their money and hid it under their mattresses. As Dandelion famously said, "We made the money on a mattress and it's only fitting we save our money under a mattress."

I can say with complete veracity that Hyrum's relations with the young ladies was strictly business — and I assure the world that this is true as well for me. They were like sisters to me and as daughters to Hyrum. And they were fun to be with—the Del Mar/Monte was a business success because the secret of a

---

[47] Enrico Honore died in 1862; Carolina Honore in 1875. They were married 41 years. C.H. said he was aware of only one time he heard his parents having a "serious" argument. It ended when Enrico declared, "You will never find a man as good as me." To which Carolina replied: "I can kick a piece of shit, and 50 men better than you will come from out of it."

[48] I have seen those accounts, preserved as historic documents, bearing the impressive seal of the Great Western Bank—which went belly up in the Great Depression of 1873 (not to be confused with the Panic of 1893). The '73 crash was caused by railroad speculation.

successful life is happiness. To be happy one need only get in the habit of acting happy. Soon the "acting" becomes reality. These are Hyrum's words. He said that when we get up in the morning we have a choice of clothing to wear — and a choice of whether to put on a happy face or a sad face.

It was Hyrum's philosophy that unhappiness is merely an excuse for failure, and while we are alive we want no reminder that we are all bound for ultimate defeat. Life, he pointed out, has a built-in tragedy.

"Do you believe in an afterlife?" I asked.

"Certainly," he answered. "Death should be viewed with dignity and a great sense of adventure."

"Everything is an adventure to you," I said.

He answered: "Thank you."

Hyrum was the second philosopher I had met in San Francisco. The first was the Celestial who had served up those two bowls of white rice in my first minutes in San Francisco. Although we did not exchange one word I sensed a fatalistic bent to his soul.

"He viewed life from the opposite pole from your philosophy," I said to Hyrum. "He said to slide along with nature, that nature — fate — was all powerful...."

"Ah," said Hyrum, "you were impressed by the serenity of our Chinese friends. Let me admit to you that at first I toyed with the idea of offering the Vista Del Mar commission to a Celestial, but decided against it. Do you know why?"

"I don't suppose you speak Chinese," I said.

Burgundia, whose habit it was to sit across the room with a book on her lap monitoring our conversations — whether it be on the practical subject of moving the Del Mar or the impractical subject of Chinese philosophy, chimed in, "Don't bet on it."

"We Caucasians — and this is doubly true of the Del Mar girls — are poisoned with a race superiority that does not allow us to learn from a more patient people. The Celestial is discreet, resigned. He accepts life as it is.

"But, alas! We are Westerners. We challenge our environment. Someday we shall change it. Someday we shall conquer death. In the meantime, do this test: In Monterey there is a Chinese whorehouse. Make inquiry...."

Burgundia sat up. She appeared agitated. "Inquiry doesn't mean you go into that place," she said. A choir of a thousand angels could not have produced music sweeter than her proprietary exclamation.

"...make inquiry," Hyrum continued, "of those who frequent both establishments. You will find that good humor and confidence of the Del Mar girls tops the resignation and passiveness of the Lotus Leaf."

The conversation had settled heavily on the carnal and away from the original proposition, i.e. Hyrum had decided against hiring a Celestial to move the Del Mar because...??? I was anxious to go back to it out of respect for Burgundia's presence in the room. Frankly, this "openness" among members of this family was at first startlingly refreshing but at other times, as was the case at hand, disconcerting.[49]

"I decided against a Chinese because of the Del Mar ladies' profound prejudice against foreigners," he explained. "The Del Mar ladies are bigoted in favor of the hairy Westerner. You see, socially they are at the hardscrabble bottom of our societal barrel. They must have someone to look down upon, ergo the Celestial. In our great cities in the East, the street sweeper can look down on the sewer worker. The sewer worker, with no one to look down upon, ends up killing himself."

"Daddy," cried Burgundia, "That's not so."

Hyrum chuckled. "Of course it isn't."

---

[49] According to C.H. after Aunt Della took the novice veil her mother, Mary Lawrence, insisted that Hyrum "clean up his act." At first Hyrum resisted, declaring, "It's not an act." To which his wife replied: "Everything you do is an act."

3

On to Monterey

I left San Francisco in the pre-dawn blackness of late August 1849.[50] I had two mounts, both midnight blacks, which I alternately rode and packed. I carried no weapon save a skinning knife, and, outwardly, my only possessions of value were my horses of which California had aplenty.

My road took me to the mission[51] situated in a small fertile plain embosomed among gentle, green clad hills. Several tiny rivulets of clear, sweet water met about the spot and proceeded to the bay in one larger stream.[52] I was the only non-cleric to join the Padres at early mass.

I walked to the altar rail to receive the sacrament of communion out of habit, having dismissed my sin with Mabel Clark, and perhaps a much greater sin that will be attached to Hyrum Milton's job of work.

What I really wanted to do at the altar is ask God to allow my love for Burgundia Milton to flower. I asked the Lord's

---

[50] He does not give an exact date because, I believe, his chronology is a bit off. The question is: how many days did he spend at Hyrum Milton's home preparing for the Del Mar move? And in his narrative does he then leave enough time to get to the California State Constitutional Convention in Monterey? My best guess is that he started off on his "curious enterprise" on August 18. We are stuck with an author who very much believes in "poetic license."

[51] St. Francis of Asís, dedicated by Fr. Francisco Palóu on June 29, 1776. A fire destroyed the original mission, and a new church was dedicated in 1791. At the time C.H. was there, wood clapboard sidings were applied to the original adobe walls. A few years later two plank roads linked downtown San Francisco and the mission.

[52] Mission Creek.

protection against thieves, although I had to admit that a thief who caused this whorehouse odyssey to be aborted would truly be doing God's work. I asked God to comfort my parents. I asked that my horses have an easy time of it.[53]

When I left the church it was barely daylight, the world engulfed in a heavy fog. "Keep me healthy, Christ!" I shouted into the fog. A voice—definitely not Christ's—answered: "I'll give it a try, but I'm only human."

Thus it was that I met the grandest friend a man has ever had, although we were in each other's company only for the week it took us to get to Monterey, the month we spent in that town going about our separate duties, and again in later years when he returned to California to be honored and celebrated as the greatest travel writer of that age.[54]

---

[53] In California at this time, no one paid more than an ounce of gold ($16) for a horse. In Spanish California, horses were so plentiful riders on long treks would literally run their mounts to death.

[54] Unfortunately, I will have to burst another of C.H.'s bubbles regarding his celebrated friend. Because both my father and I bear Bayard Taylor's name a lengthy footnote is in order. B.T. was born January 11, 1825, in Kennett Square, Pennsylvania. He rebelled at the deadly quiet of his Quaker village upbringing. When B.T. was 14, Thomas Dunn English (author of *Ben Bolt* but at that time a practicing physician-phrenologist) read the bumps on B.T.'s head and declared he was destined to be a "traveler" and a "poet." With tremendous determination the 14-year-old bent his ambition in these two directions. ¶ In 1842, B.T. was apprenticed as a printer to the West Chester *Record* and he had a poem published in the *Saturday Evening Post*. Rufus Wilmot Griswold, American anthologist, editor, poet, and critic took an interest in B.T. and made it possible for him to spend two years (1844-46) in Europe as a correspondent for three publications. The freshness and spontaneity of his early travel pieces caught the public's fancy and he became a sort of "American Marco Polo." In New York he taught school and became literary editor of the *Tribune*. ¶ He spent five months in California, then returned to the East where he married Mary Agnew, a Quaker girl from his home town. She died two months later of tuberculosis. B.T. spent the next two years on a voyage around the world. He was with Commodore Perry as a master's mate when Japan was opened to the West. In 1857 he married Marie Hansen, daughter of the Danish astronomer and herself a writer and translator. They had one child, a daughter. In 1858 B.T. bought a farm, *Cedarcroft*, near Kennett Square, but his hometown bored him. In order to

Out of the fog, afoot, with pack on his back, emerged a young,55 lean man dressed from head to boot-top in fresh corduroy. He had a generous head and hanging wetly down the sides of it, under a floppy hat, were strands of carrot-colored hair.

Bayard Taylor was in California as the special correspondent of the *New York Herald*. He had come to these Pacific shores, via the Isthmus of Panama, to report on the California Constitutional Convention in order to satisfy a growing legion of Eastern readers nearly all of whom either had a relative, friend, or someone they knew was in California picking up gold nuggets.

Had Bayard been a dishonest reporter, I am sure he could have returned home with pockets full of gold, but he chose to tell the truth about some of the Golden State's not-so-golden attributes. This gave the Southern States enough excuse to delay admittance of still another Free State for precious months pending further compromise on the way to the Civil War. There were Northerners, also, in the Senate not exactly captivated with the new Western Empire recently acquired from Mexico.[56]

---

make ends meet, he had to distill more writings and lectures from his travels. Parke Godwin, the editor and writer, said Taylor had "traveled more and seen less than any man living."¶ In 1862 B.T. was appointed secretary of the U.S. legation at St. Petersburg. He translated Faust in the original meters. From 1870 to 1877 he was professor of German literature at Cornell. B.T.'s fame was like a comet — for a while it outshown the sun, but it was brief. He lost his money; returned to the *Tribune* and endless travel. In 1878 he was appointed minister to Germany. He died in December of that year. Everything about B.T.'s work and life was hollow. "The brilliance of his life," wrote Carl Van Doran, "...blinded men to the mediocrity of his actual achievements." He was the "laureate of the gilded age." He himself was gilded and not gold — in complete accord with his age. "A life of Bayard Taylor," wrote one critic, "is a history and indictment of America in the mid-19th Century."

[55] B.T. was 25.

[56] C.H.'s history is a mite simplistic. The Compromise of 1850 was a package of five separate bills passed by Congress in September 1850, which defused a four-year political confrontation between slave and free states regarding the status of territories acquired from Mexico.

"Four hostile newspapers are more to be feared than a thousand bayonets," said the Great Bonaparte. Bayard was not "hostile" — he was honest — which means the greedy and the stupid had more to fear from his pen than they did two thousand bayonets. A blithe heart makes a blooming visage, and my friend has lighted the back rooms of my memory from that far-away day to this.

"Where are you heading?" Bayard asked after critically sizing-up the earthly petitioner standing in a pool of embarrassment before him.

"Monterey," I said. "And you?"

"Monterey, also," he said, adding: "Are you a delegate?"

Bayard was a recognized talent. No greater crown can be placed upon the brow of a young man. He was happy in his work, and the direct inspiration for this history — but I must add in haste that my humble efforts are in no way to be regarded in the same vein as the outpourings of a Bayard Taylor. From Bayard's stay in California came the book *El Dorado*.[57]

The most precious personal correspondence I have, with the exception of Burgundia's tender will,[58] is a "private" letter Bayard wrote to me explaining why he made no mention of my "curious enterprise" in *El Dorado*: "You trusted the one person who could have broadcast the details of your extraordinary mission to the far corners of the literate world." He extracted from me a promise to "someday write it all down to give a full and human dimension to the story of California."

Regarding the writing of this journal: I must confess — I am an incorrigible plagiarist. I use plagiarism even to describe my weakness. I steal sweet and honeyed sentences, but borrowed garments never keep one warm enough. To put it simply: I

---

[57] Taylor returned home by way of Mexico. Within two weeks of release, his two-volume *El Dorado; or, Adventures in the Path of Empire*, sold 10,000 copies in the United States and 30,000 in Great Britain.

[58] Nana preceded C.H. in death by a year. Her will was a straightforward legal document.

am not a writer. I have no desire to be remembered as one. This biography is the payment of a debt I owe for my good fortune. Nothing will please my dust more than to have some pup lard his lean book with whatever fat he finds in this work. Our poets steal from Homer. Our story-dressers do as much. He that comes last is commonly best.[59]

Bayard and I proceeded together, each on horseback after redistributing the pack supplies, through the fog-shrouded sandhills, emerging in sunlight in the San Mateo region stretching south from San Francisco to create the peninsula.[60]

Our road—El Camino Real—followed the bayside flatlands. It was rutted and completely unmarked, but at every crossroad, as fortune dictated, there was a habitation or a native or a fellow traveler from whom we received a point down the "Monterey Road."

What exhilaration I felt on that open road. As nature gives liberty even to dumb animals,[61] it was not the freedom from master or parent that made my blood sing; it was more: the May of life only blooms once, and I, to my everlasting profit, was aware of it.

We slept under the stars, which gave me the chance to recall my final day at Hyrum Milton's home—and Burgundia. This closing scene is etched in my soul:

Hyrum was gone from the room when Burgundia entered.

"Is Daddy here?" she asked, wide-eyed as usual.

"No, Burgundia," I replied. "He's been called away."

"You don't talk much, do you," she said.

"Not much."

"Are you shy or just don't have much to say?"

"I'm shy around you."

This stopped her. I was paying her a compliment. My hope

---

[59] Where to start? Most of these declarations are "borrowed" from Robert Burton.

[60] First C.H. tells us he is no writer, then he proves it with this 34-word sentence.

[61] A quote from Tacitus.

was that she would accept in.

"Are you coming back to San Francisco?" she asked.

"Why...."

"I mean after you go gold digging in Sonora. Most young men come out here to dig for gold."

"I like to think I'm not like 'most young men'."

Her guard down, she blurted: "You're not."

"Thank you," I said.

"I mean most young men go from one camp to another until they get so sick of California and its gold, they hurry home as fast as they can."

She circled around my chair as she spoke until I held out my hand and stopped her. "You seem to know a great deal about 'young men'," I said. "Are you interested in young men?"

My question did not faze her. She snapped: "Aren't you interested in young women?"

"Burgundia," I said, "would you like me to write[62] to you from Monterey and Sonoran Camp?"

Her reply was instantaneous and startling: Falling to her knees, she took hold of my hand, fluttered her eye lashes, and emoted with all the fervor of a bad actress in a bad play: "Oh, yes! Yes! Yes! I shall hardly be able to draw a breath until I can tear open your envelope to read your deathless description of the Journey of the Vista Del Mar!"

Then she threw back her head and laughed so loud and long that I thought she was in danger of bursting a blood vessel. Then I remembered: I had heard her father do such uncontrollable roaring when he told of a poor soul who was a coffin maker always trying to pass himself off as a cabinet maker. It was basic to the Miltons.[63]

When she recovered she was on her way out the door. "I'm sorry," she said pausing to make her exit, "I'd like it very

---

[62] All the letters between C.H. and Nana Burgundia were neatly stored in two drawers of a tall lacquered Chinese lingerie chest.

[63] It skipped Zinfandella; I do not know about Champagnes.

much if you would write."

At *El Pueblo de San José*[64] Bayard and I took some time off to do a bit of exploring — Bayard concentrating on the people, me on the old adobes of the two missions in this vicinity: San José and Santa Clara. Some very gracious Californios, Andreas Pacheco and his wife, Maria,[65] gave us supper and a bed to sleep in. They sent their sons to take care of our horses, saying extra caution was needed because several grizzly bears had been seen at their usual dining spot, the place a mile north of the town where cattle were slaughtered and their hides[66] removed.

Before I tell of the next incident, let me reassure you that the Mexican horseman is without equal in the world. It is said with a great deal of truth that the Mexican infant can ride a horse before he can walk. The Mexican having a task to perform 50 yards from where he is standing will whistle for his horse to come to him rather than walk the 50 yards. Thus it was just before dusk settled in that we heard the most God-dreadful commotion — screams, shrieks, laughter, cries, pounding hooves — coming down the street toward the Pacheco homestead. The two boys charged with "taking care" of our horses had decided to ride them to the bone yard, lasso a grizzly bear, and haul him screaming and bellowing down the street for the general amusement of the neighbors.

"Tonight the pueblo will have some bear meat to eat," Andreas Pacheco said.

---

[64] Founded in 1777.

[65] One of my grandson duties for C.H. was to deliver Christmas Packages to the Pachecos and a long list of others in the Bay Area. One of their sons, Hermano, managed C.H.'s rancho in the south end of the Santa Clara Valley near what is today the city of Gilroy. That property was deeded to Hermano at C.H.'s death in 1913.

[66] In pre-United States days, California's chief export was hides — known as "California Dollar Bills." Yankee ships would bring the manufactured largess of the East Coast to the padres, ranchers, and citizens of California, and return with their holds full of dried cow hides. These became shoes, some of which were sold back to the California Hispanics, who never bothered to learn the shoemaker's craft.

"It takes weeks for the meat to hang so one can chew it," his practical wife said. "We will give the gentleman a haunch so they can enjoy the meat later."

Before we departed San José we stopped by a particular farmhouse recommended by our hosts to satisfy Bayard's need to meet some of the local inhabitants. It was here we met a young girl, Virginia Reed, who would be regarded in later years as one of California's most famous curiosities.

She was the "midnight heroine" of the Donner Party.[67] The great tragedy of the winter of 1846-47, in which an emigrant party was trapped by snow in the Sierras, involved cannibalism. As one can imagine this caused a sensation.[68]

San José and the Santa Clara Valley was a garden paradise that Bayard would extol in his published writings. Traveling

---

[67] C.H. manufactured this meeting out of whole cloth. Bayard Taylor does not mention it in *El Dorado*. When Virginia's step-father was banished from the main Donner camp for murdering John Snyder, young Virginia went out at night to take food, a gun, and arrows to him.

[68] C.H. and Bayard spent a second night in San José, the narrative of which does not appear in the final draft of his memoirs, nor does he give the thoughts that caused him "to chuckle" at the Stevens Creek camp. To make his story complete, I insert them here: ¶ Stevens Creek: "This memory causes me to chuckle because my grandson, a clever fellow, quit his law studies at the school [Stanford University] that would be built here, and became a wood-chopper. He is the third and probably the last philosopher of my acquaintance, he having taken Voltaire to heart regarding the need for one to 'tend his own garden.'" ¶ Second day in San José: "Bayard had business in town. He was going to meet Col. Charles Fremont, the 'Pathfinder.' I wandered about the sleepy pueblo plaza. A lean Yankee, with yellow parchment for skin, was conducting an open-air auction by waving a cheap knife under the noses of a half-dozen onlookers, and chanting a liturgy that had a hypnotic effect even on those who understood no English: '...this fine knife was made under an Act of Congress at the rate of thirty-six dollars per dozen...a blade that even your wife can wield...it will cut cast-iron steam steel or bone and will stick a frog, hog, toad or the devil's tail and has a spring on it like a mule's hind leg....' As Bayard and the Pathfinder were going to sup together that evening, I wandered into a fandango hall whose main feature was an oily plank resting on two barrels behind which sat the musicians. There were two of them—the meanest looking Mexicans ever placed in tandem. Where the guitar player did not have a knife scar upon

south from San José down the broad valley, we stole away from the peopled world to enter a hazy day that all but obscured the parallel mountains hedging the valley. Our road was perfectly level, and it passed through wide reaches of grazing land occasionally interrupted by park-like tracts, studded with oaks and sycamores — a charming interchange of scenery.[69] We crossed the dry bed of Coyote Creek several times and reached Capt. Fisher's Ranche as it was growing dusk. A passing traveler warned us to look out for bears. Capt. Fisher's ranch consisted of foursquare leagues of land — about 18,000 acres. He purchased the spread at auction in 1846 for $3000, which was then considered a high price, but since the discovery of gold he has been offered $80,000 for it — a familiar California success story. Real estate has made more geniuses in California than has its universities.

Capt. Fisher reaffirmed Bayard's first impressions of California being an agricultural country. The barren, burnt appearance of the plains during the summer season misled many as to the true value of this country.

"All California needs is water to make it fruitful," the good captain said.

"That's all hell needs," I said silently to myself.[70]

Next day we continued our southward journey through the sea of wild grain. At Murphy's Ranche[71] we met a Mr.

his exposed flesh, the mandolin player did. The patrons, to a man, turned to look me over. Each and every person in that room had spent at least a lifetime out of range of a wash tub."

[69] C.H. takes his description of the Santa Clara Valley and of Fisher's Ranch from *El Dorado*.

[70] I'm sure by now readers of this memoir are anxious to get to Monterey and Hyrum Milton's whorehouse, but we should round out our California picture by quoting Bayard Taylor's take on the state's agriculture potential: "Corn grows upon the plains...it requires no irrigation, and is not planted until after the last rain has fallen. Vegetables thrive luxuriantly, and many species, such as melons, pumpkins, squashes, beans, potatoes, etc., require no further care than the planting. Grape vines in some situations require to be occasionally watered; when planted on moist slopes, they produce without it. A Frenchman named

Ruckel of San Francisco, and a Mr. Everett of New York, who were rusticating a few days in the neighborhood. Mr. Murphy, our host, a native of Ireland who had come to California in 1843, owned nine leagues of land in the center of Santa Clara Valley. I often wonder if his boyhood chums back in the old country could comprehend the fact of nine leagues of land.[72] Lowborn Murphy owning that much land? Impossible.[73]

Behind the ranch is a distinctive peak[74] to which we rode the next day in company with Mr. Murphy. Spread out before us was the grand panorama of the oak and grain carpeted land.

At dinner that night our circle was increased by the arrival of a Catholic missionary from Oregon. He brought fresh details of the Indian massacre the previous winter. When he learned my destination was Sonoran Camp (but not my purpose in going there), he warned me to stay clear of the Oregonians who were hell-bent on avenging the Whitman massacre victims by killing any Indian of any age or sex

---

Vigne made 100 barrels of wine in one year from a vineyard of about six acres, which he cultivated at the Mission San José. Capt. Fisher had a thousand vines in his garden, which were leaning on the earth from the weight of their fruit.

[71] At the present site of Morgan Hill.

[72] There is no universally accepted measurement of a league. Originally it was the distance a person could walk in an hour—three miles. In Murphy's case, C.H. penciled in a note in the margin: "Nine leagues: 40,000 acres."

[73] This very incident happened to C.H. in 1872 when he and Nana Burgundia went to Italy to visit aunts, uncles, nephews, nieces, and cousins. These people were curious about America and they asked pointed questions. When he told them his ranch at Santa Rosa was 18,000 acres, one of the younger mavericks all but called him a liar. And this accusation was confirmed when C.H. said his cattle gave birth in the wild instead of in the ground floor paddock atop which are the living quarters of every cattle owner in Italy.

[74] This is properly Murphy's Peak, not, as commonly supposed, the "hill" in Morgan Hill. Morgan Hill is the first and last name of a man who bought and subdivided this land.

encountered in the diggings.[75] (Did he mistake me for an Indian?)

Early the next day we were at the *Las Animas*[76] rancho, the site today of New Gilroy. In 1812 an English sailor named John Gilroy jumped ship in Monterey and made his way to this place where he married the daughter of the owner of this rancho—the definitive "rags to riches" tale—one day confined to the cramped hold of a odoriferous British merchantman on hardtack and moldy corned beef, the next lord of 14,000 bountiful acres of California land plus the bonus of a warm and attractive senorita in your bed.

I know the area well for one of my sons settled there.[77] Bayard Taylor took advantage of our location among some townspeople by conducting some interviews. The testimony of one very disgruntled "emigrant"—a haggard woman lately from Tennessee. She greeted us with, "Them black horses look sickly. You're welcome to rest up your animals, but the fleas will eat you alive."

Our horses were not "sickly" nor had we encountered fleas in the Santa Clara Valley. She went on: "No bears or Indians in these parts, but we get worse—malaria."

By her account her husband had "dragged" her to

---

[76] Actually the *San Ysidro* grant of 14,000 acres.

[77] My uncle Milton Hyrum Honore (1853-1912) is that son. He moved to New Gilroy to cultivate the tobacco leaf industry, which bloomed briefly then gave way to the prune industry. He had four children: Theresa, Peter, Louisa, and Enrico (Harry). A second uncle, Caesar Honore Jr. died in infancy. My aunt Jeanne Honore Koki (1854-1931) married a Japanese diplomat and lived mostly in Europe. She had three children, Giacinto, Michael, and Louisa. My father, Bayard Taylor Honore Sr. (1854-1899), had three children: Richard, Eugene, and me. My two brothers eschewed the family business and instead tried to make a mark in burlesque as comics. There followed a long series of make-overs, notably "The Butterfinger Jugglers," "The World's Smartest Horse," and "Tap Dancing Fools." My father managed the family business briefly until his untimely death at age 45 in a railroad derailment near Sargent south of Gilroy. Coincidently, Sargent is my mother's maiden name. She was born in 1862 and passed away in 1928.

California "by the scruff of my neck." And, the sing-song lament: "My how I miss Tennessee—all green and full of water and kindly folks." Then her tune changed: "Of course when all that green turns to ash we'll see how kindly some of them uppity scoundrels will be."

Then: "What's your business in Monterey? Politics, I wager." Politics, indeed. Bayard told her we were journalists (I had been promoted!) on our way to report on the constitutional convention (and other matters I said to myself).

"California ain't worth one drop of blood spilt over her," she said. "You two don't strike me as a pair who spill much sweat for your bread."

And then: "Bread! I ain't seen a decent peck of wheat flour since I turned my back on Tennessee."[78]

Ever southward, our next "hotel" was the Mission San Juan Bautista situated on a rise in the center of a bowl-like valley. We arrived as the vespers were tinkling into the dusk.

There were many Indians about. These were the Missionized Costanoans, a peaceful folk now bewildered by the white man's desire to "save" their souls while, at the same time, making use of their muscles.

At the day school I attended in Boston I early recognized that my Latin countenance was different from the blonde, blue-eyed norm displayed by my classmates. I yearned not to be different. But, later, after I was exposed to the history of the Romans and their achievements, I took pride in the fact that while my ancestors were building aqueducts and entertaining guests at lavish banquets, the ancestors of these fair-heads

---

[78] C.H. told me he had a vivid memory of this woman—a "croaker" he labeled her. It must have been catching for in 1857 when the Butterfield Stage line added the final link to the Atlantic-to-Pacific road, *New York Herald* correspondent Waterman Ormsby, the only passenger on the 24-day ride from St. Louis to San Francisco, reported the citizens at every stop were effusive in their praise of this monumental achievement—except in Gilroy. A citizen of that town—"the only croaker I met from St. Louis to San Francisco"—told Ormsby the transcontinental service wasn't "such a big much," for mail or for people.

were painting their naked bodies with blue stripes and scouring the wilds for wild garlic, nettles and watercress.

What in his past can the Indian point to with pride? He has no aqueducts or coliseums, only centuries of peaceful, independent existence. That fool of a historian Bancroft paints a vile picture of these maligned first Californians.[79]

Leaving San Juan uncharacteristically at noon because Bayard had a morning appointment with an emigrant who had mastered passage to California via the Gila (Southern) Trail, we crossed a spur and descended into the plain of the Salinas River. There was considerable traffic both heading to and from the direction of Monterey. When we came at last to the sound of the surf beating on the coastline, we went our separate ways.[80] This was my idea. The *New York Herald* would find little profit if it became known that one of their correspondents had partnered-up with a whorehouse relocator.

Although ours had been a leisurely stroll from San Francisco to Monterey, I felt hardened by the trek. I felt alive and reinvigorated, but I did not want to present myself to the Vista Del Mar ladies in my soiled clothing and equally soiled body. The hotel rooms would all be filled with convention folks as would be all the beds-for-hire in private homes. Bayard had made prior arrangements and he had lodging. I could not barge in on him. As to the Vista Del Mar, I knew I would be able to fight off any temptation I might have by way of things à la Mabel Clark, but one 20-year-old man and seven very experienced females could be, if I can rightly remember

---

[79] For instance, Bancroft asserts Indians have an easy time of childbirth because they mated, like animals, in season. Hubert Bancroft was a book seller who took to hiring young writers to work in his San Francisco mill turning out prodigious amounts of fact and fiction to which Bancroft affixed his name. C.H. fought to keep Bancroft's books out of the libraries that the Honore family might be financing.

[80] C.H. does not relate how or if they dealt with the pack horse Bayard was riding.

my Latin, *molestus*.[81]

And, of course, there was Burgundia.

I left the main road and turned directly west for the sea. A roaring bonfire soon came into view to direct me to a group of men standing around the fire discussing — politics! I was safe. These men were not cutthroats in the literal sense. That is they might crush you with unvarnished rhetoric, but no knives would be flashed, and there would be no blood.

One fellow stood apart, opening fancy looking tins of food for his evening mess. The name of the American aristocrat was Zachary Fenner. He was dressed as per an appearance before a British Lord Chamberlin, and, I was to learn later, exactly fitted for that role.[82] His horse had drowned in a quicksand bog on the shoreline just a few hours before. He tried to buy a horse from the assembled politicians, with no luck.

I knew who this fellow was, not from his physical appearance (I had never laid eyes on him prior to this very moment), not from his attire, not from his having steered his poor horse into a deadly sink-hole. It was from his food tins! In telling me about Zachary Fenner, Hyrum Milton said that they had been together in the import food market when a box of *pate de foie gras* was opened on arrival and Fenner bought the whole lot. When the patrons present voiced objection, Fenner offered to sell them a tin or two from his horde — at double what he paid.

Fenner's interest in Monterey was not to report on the convention, but to learn what he could of the soundness of rumors concerning Hyrum Milton. Fenner was retained by San Francisco interests politically hostile to my employer and

---

[81] Troublesome.

[82] I believe what C.H. refers to is the historic role of the Lord Chamberlin dating back to the Licensing Act of 1737. This gave the Lord Chamberlin statutory authorization to veto the appearance of any play performed in the United Kingdom. One need not strain the brain to figure out what this official might think about whorehouses.

patron. Recognizing the *pate de foie gras* gave me a strategic advantage.

"What's your business in Monterey?" my new campmate asked, much in the same tone of voice one would ask a dog why it was leaving the warmth of a fireside. "Most of the young men your age are heading in the other direction—to the gold diggings."

"I've had my fill of gold digging," I said. I added nothing more to that dishonest statement. Then I took the offensive.

"What brings you to Monterey?" I asked, with no expectation of his telling the truth.

"Business," he answered.

And so we folded up our imaginary chess board, spread our canvas covers, and went to sleep to the tune of the politicians at the bonfire arguing the fine points of democracy.

4

The Vista Del Mar

Circumstance dictated that I find the Vista Del Mar on my own steam. Monterey is nestled between two low green hills overlooking a crescent-shaped bay. Although not a quarter the size of San Francisco in population, its tile-roofed white adobes were more solidly built. Some of the Monterey adobe residences were actually elegant in their symmetry and spaciousness.

The town's aspect was quiet and strictly Spanish. I saw several *Dons* clothed in the *serape* and *calcineros*, walking the streets with lordly airs, and pretty *senoritas*, dark eyes peering through the folds of their *rebosos*, skipping lightly along the footpaths, always under the watchful eye of an elderly chaperone entrusted to guard the family's most valuable asset: the virginity of the carefree, as of now at least, young girls.[83]

There were seven ships anchored in the bay (San Francisco Bay held upwards to 700). The American flag danced in the steady breeze atop the fort on the bluff: a neat and spacious Presidio of yellow stone—a distinguishing feature of the landscape, and certainly not the "height" I was told the Vista Del Mar occupied.

I concentrated on the road leading to the Mission Carmel,

---

[83] A culture that urges every young man to prove his manhood by the quantity, not so much the quality, of his conquests and commands that very same Lothario defend the family's honor by killing any man who defiles his sister makes for some interesting social dynamics.

steering clear of the plaza and the Town Hall[84] where the new state's business will be conducted tomorrow. I tethered my horses in a livery and found on the outskirts an eating establishment. (Bayard, I was to learn later, was billeted at the Presidio cuartel.[85]) I was famished and for one of Hyrum Milton's dollars I was served by the cook's *muchacho* an *olla* of boiled beef, cucumbers, corn, an *asado* of beef and red peppers, a *guisado* of beef and potatoes, and all the coffee needed to wash it all down.

The best part of the day lay ahead of me when I took to the road that led up to the pine-dotted heights — the ideal setting for a Chinese lacquer house.

Years later, remembering that climb up that gentle slope, through the mist of the days and months and years between, I most vividly recall the wonderful tonic of youth — the certainty that life is everlasting.[86]

With each step I took the problems I conjured at the restaurant regarding my mission slid from my mind as sand

[84] Renamed Colton Hall after Rev. Walter Colton, a Yale graduate who came to Monterey as chaplain aboard Commodore Robert Field Stockton's ship. Colton was *alcalde* of Monterey. He wrote a great deal of the gold rush. A sample: "The gold mines are producing one good result; every creditor who has gone there is paying his debts...this has rendered the credit of every man here good for almost any amount. Orders for merchandise are honored which six months ago would have been thrown in the fire...the only capital required is muscle and an honest purpose...I met a man today (September 16, 1848) from the mines in patched buckskin, rough as a badger from his hole, who had $15,000 in yellow dust swung at his back. Talk to him of brooches gold-headed canes and carpenter's coats! Why he can unpack a lump of gold that would throw all Chestnut Street into spasms.... His rights in the great domain are equal to yours...he bends the knee to no man...clear out of the way with your crests, and crowns and pedigree trees and let this democrat pass. Every drop of blood in his veins tells that it flows from a great heart which God has made and which man shall never enslave. Such are the genuine sons of California; such may they live and die.

[85] Soldiers' barracks.

[86] I was 26 years old when C.H. died. His final words to me in the hospital where he lay dying were: "Get the hell out of this place. Don't come back."

slips through a glass. The dripping pine forest, hung with gray-green Spaniard's Beard, gave a mystic quality to this setting. The tide pools below on the shoreline were filled with the unseen life of the sea, but the forest flaunted that life: a strange counterweight to the life I felt within my being as I moved through the lush vegetation.

Youth and freedom. I had two of God's most precious gifts. Up to my San Francisco arrival, I enjoyed the comfort of being dependent—my parents, my schoolmasters, Lord John-Cowe, and, for that matter, Hyrum Milton. Now I was away from all of them, miles away. And then an errant thought: If I were to win Burgundia would I not again be dependent on another?

The Vista Del Mar came into view. It was low and rambling (each girl did business in her own room, if not her "castle" at least her sacrosanct turret). The exterior showed the incredible workmanship of the Chinese craftsmen and artists who fashioned and decorated this misnamed palace. Every detail—every finial, every overhang, every railing, every shelf, every sill harmonized with the whole.[87]

Even my untrained eye could see how this puzzle-box was assembled and how it would be unassembled then reassembled in Sonoran Camp.

After standing in awe at the stone gate leading to the entrance my thoughts shifted to the seven occupants in residence here. These demimondes would naturally object to leaving the peaceful Monterey environs for the storm of a gold camp, not just any gold camp but one in which

---

[87] C.H. commanded the construction of many commercial and residential structures. He would review architectural submissions with a pen in hand, striking out details that merely added to form and not function. The first thing to go was the decorated column which supported thin air. He was forever lecturing architects in his belief that the folk preferred form over function. "People care more about how a thing looks than how it works," he would say. "That's why they are the folk."

foreigners[88] were dominant. But, that problem, if indeed it occurred, would be solved by Hyrum according to Hyrum's sacred conviction that every move in life is governed by an organism choosing the path that promises the most gain and the least loss. In other words, the ladies would be swayed by the almighty dollar.

Hyrum had the means to hire an army to perfect this transfer of property, yet he hired a lone soldier. An untried soldier, inexperienced soldier at that. Why? Even if more than a growing fondness between Burgundia and me had been noticed, surely that would not have caused him to give me this job.[89]

But, far be it for me to wonder at Hyrum's tactics or motives. Tomorrow was a sacred promise, but only the young have tomorrow. How unkind toward my elders was that declaration. How unkind in general is youth toward the elderly. How resentful are the aged toward the young.[90]

With this bit of philosophizing behind me, I gave the clapper a couple of raps, which in a short time produced the sound of shuffling. Then the sound of a panel sliding open, then sliding shut. More shuffling. Finally a feminine voice: "It's him."

---

[88] Up until the signing of the Treaty of Peace, Friendship, Limits and Settlement Between the United States of America and the Mexican Republic at Guadalupe Hidalgo on February 2, 1848, the Americans were the "foreigners" and the Mexicans the native born citizens of Alta California.

[89] I asked both of my grandparents this question. C.H.'s answer was, "Don't play poker, Bayard, you wouldn't be good at it." Nana Burgundia said, "I tried to mask my feelings for Caesar, but I guess I didn't fool Daddy."

[90] The "natural conflict" between the young and old was a frequent subject at C.H.'s dinner table. He often cited the paradox in Shakespeare's *Romeo and Juliet* — the young lovers, with the years stretching beyond them, in a mad rush to consummate their love; the old parents and the friar — with only weeks and months remaining, preaching caution and restraint.

IT'S HIM? I marveled at Hyrum's efficiency. He had preceded me with word to the Vista Del Mar not only who I was, but what I looked like.[91]

A Sancho Panza-like character[92] appeared at the far corner of the house, motioning me to follow him to what I assumed was the "servant's entrance." (I later learned that this gentleman went by the name "Professor.")

Dandelion, all smiles, met me in what turned out to be the kitchen: "Welcome, Caesar...."

She mispronounced my name: "It's CHEZari," I said.

One by one the young ladies appeared, in various costumes apropos to their trade.

Dandelion explained Rick Brazelton's absence. He was scouting the countryside for wagons and teams of horses to buy—Hyrum Milton again running the show.

---

[91] It was Mary Lawrence Milton who supplied those details.
[92] C.H. held that the only Spanish literature worth reading was Cervantes and his *Don Quixote*.

5

Introducing the Cast

Nine is an over much of characters to introduce all at once in a memoir, but nine there were: the two men attached to the Vista Del Mar, and the seven young ladies who made it go.

The Professor you have met briefly. Pablo Perez was from Hermosillo in the Free and Sovereign State of Sonora. He was a placer miner, one of hundreds from Sonora, Republic of Mexico, who taught the gringos where to find pay-dirt and how to separate out the gold from the gravel. Why he left Sonoran Camp for Monterey is his secret, and why he wanted to return to that place is likewise his secret.

Rick Brazelton, a lieutenant of dragoons under General Stephen Watts Kearny, left three fingers and the palm of his left hand at San Pasqual.[93] After he was mustered out he tried gold mining for a while then he "raised a little hell in San Francisco" which caused him to come under the "jurisdiction" of Judge Hyrum Milton. Brazelton was "paroled to keep the peace" at the Vista Del Mar. His "bonus" pay included a go at all the girls, but when he found he was becoming emotionally as well as physically involved with members of his "harem," he gave up sex, cigars, whiskey and — as a final

---

[93] Kearny had started west at the head of an army bound to take California. After pacifying New Mexico, he learned from Kit Carson, Fremont's scout, that California had been taken by Fremont and Commodore Stockton without much of a struggle. Kearney sent the bulk of his force back east, and persuading a reluctant Carson to turn around and guide his token force to California, started off for the Pacific. At San Pasqual the resurrected *Californios* gave the American force a sound trouncing.

sacrifice — beer.[94]

The 23-year-old Dandelion was the "boss lady." She was a handsome young woman, but her body was perhaps a trifle less womanly soft than the vast areas of exposed flesh she fancied would portend. She seldom smiled. She was "all business." And she was fiercely protective of her brood. Eight years of whoring did not crush that spark of a mother's instinct to protect her "children." She came alive while playing cards with the girls, whooping and hollering as the exposed card dictated, but she would not allow gambling.[95]

Opal[96] was 21, brunette and brown-eyed, tallish, with a fleshy torso but with thin legs and arms. She was the company's comic, and the only one of the seven who was consistently foul-mouthed. Dandelion's ban on gambling, Opal's absolute drug of choice, forced her from time to time, to spend some slack afternoons at a nearby monte saloon. If she won, she tucked the coin in her bosom; if she lost, she would invite any one with cash to join her in the liquor closet for a

---

[94] Brazelton remained friends with C.H. after the "curious enterprise" was successfully completed. He stayed on briefly in Sonora, married Scarlet, and together, with his craftsmanship and her cash, built a thriving hotel in Mariposa.

[95] Soon after the Sonora business became operative, Dandelion disappeared. Prostitutes, especially those who worked the streets, lived precarious lives. C.H. was a strong advocate of legalizing prostitution and licensing brothels as a means of providing some measure of protection for the sex workers. He cited the famous Monkey House brothel in San Francisco's Barbary Coast, the three-block area featuring dance halls, concert saloons, bars, jazz clubs, variety shows, and, of course, brothels. The Monkey House was to brothels what snipe hunting is to rubes. C.H. would describe to the uninitiated the wonders of the Monkey House: "You knock on the door and a monkey in a top hat greets you. He takes your money and leads you into a room featuring a pool table. He hands you a cue ball and a cue stick and signals for you to "break" the rack of balls. If you get one ball to fall in a pocket, you get your choice of one girl; two balls nets you two girls; three balls three girls." "What happens if you don't get any balls to fall into a pocket?" "In that case you screw the monkey!!!"

[96] Opal married a miner who hit a bonanza on the Trinity River.

replenish-the-depleted-cash-box frolic. Working off-campus was not encouraged, but when it happened, as it frequently did with Opal, the house percentage[97] was honorably paid.

Gertie, also 21, also brunette and brown-eyed, was in many respects Opal's opposite. She was short, shapely, and very emotional. A follower, uncomplaining by nature, timid, tolerant, easily upset by the unexpected appearance of a fluttering moth — or by a customer stepping out on a "nice wife and family." Gertie was the group's chief seamstress. She made the finest pleating and polonaise[98] of any busy hand in Monterey.[99]

Mary Turtle-Eyes was 19, blonde, blue-eyed, of medium stature — but her body was absolutely dazzling, especially her large and well-shaped breasts. There was nothing unusual about her eyes to warrant the "Turtle-Eyes" moniker.[100] She is best described as being kind, especially toward animals, and most especially toward cats. She kept several hot bricks on the hearth which she would strategically place around the Vista Del Mar for the comfort of her cats — until Dandelion put her foot down — literally — on a dead newborn kitten killed by a tom. The job of getting rid of the cats fell to the Professor. Mary Turtle-Eyes was disconsolate and several times went through the motion of packing her meager belongings. But, slowly the realization came to Mary that Dandelion had acted in the best interest of the Vista Del Mar and the tiny, fragile family it was home to.[101]

---

[97] 50%.

[98] A dress with an underskirt.

[99] Gertrude "Gertie" Brown met and married a Russian, discoverer of the *Burning Moscow Mine* in the Mojave Desert.

[100] As the story goes, teenage Mary Ogilbee of Patience River, Georgia, left the city, county, and state, and her teenage Negro lover left the earth via a lynching.

[101] After Sonora, Mary Turtle-eyes went to Sacramento and "Big Mary's Place." C.H., true to his "contract," helped finance the venture. After recouping his actual investment — not a penny less nor a penny more — he erased his footprints from the deal.

Daphne, 19, was the tallest of the lot, slightly awkward, even-tempered, and definitely a romantic. She read a great deal—reading that caused her to overspend on clothing. She read trash mostly, not so much for the plot melodrama but to soak up the descriptions of lavish gowns. While the other ladies answered the call of "Men in the Parlor" dressed in provocative bedroom attire, Daphne appeared as if she were on her way to a royal coronation. One of the Vista Del Mar's regulars let it be known that he would no longer choose Daphne from the parlor line-up because "It takes too damned much time to get to where I wanna go." Daphne heard about the comment and took it as a compliment. She imagined ladies undressed leisurely for the sole purpose of avoiding wrinkling their garments.[102]

Princess was a mere 17. She wore her long straight black hair pulled tightly across her skull. Her distinguishing characteristic was her bird-like mannerism—flashing black eyes darting about the room, seemingly looking for a worm to bite into. Of the lot, she was the least attractive—short and thin, yet when it came to being called out by "Men in the Parlor" she held her own. In fact she had the most exclusive "regulars." When Opal asked her for her secret, guessing Princess had an "educated pussy that sang barroom ditties," Princess answered: "I would be happy to give you lessons—for a fee, of course."[103]

---

[102] "Daphne" was Margaret Oakley of St. Joseph, Missouri. She was repeatedly raped by a cousin starting at age 12. C.H. made an effort to track down this man to bring him to justice or at least make him uncomfortable. The cousin died at a young age due to obesity. Daphne's life ended tragically.

[103] Princess, aka Prudence Sharp of Missouri, ended her Vista Del Mar days by marrying a drummer. With her earnings and a bit of help from C.H. ("Not much money," he said, "only four thousand.") she and her husband opened a dry goods store in Stockton—which has grown into the prominent Framer Hardware chain in Northern California. C.H. told me that on several occasions a Princess regular recognized the lady behind the counter.

Scarlet, the other 17-year-old, was a carrot-top, complete with green eyes. She was petite and a mite plump, serious, considerate. There was a gentility about her that reflected her upbringing by two maiden aunts. Scarlet had a passion for horses and mules—and teamsters. She was, alas, the crew's "lazy bones." "To live long," she was fond of saying, "it is necessary to live slowly." Del Mar patrons apparently did not cotton to this life style, and Scarlet had few "steadies."[104]

I was surprised to learn that "ladies-of-the-night" had "love affairs" without missing a stroke in their occupation, they being able, apparently, to separate "being in love" with "making love." They imbibed all the bad qualities of their sex when it came to their heart-directed intrigues with men.

But, in Monterey on that far-away day, they were nice girls, splendid companions, all healthy, handsome, and alive.

---

[104] But she did have the genuine love of a good man—her ticket out of the game.

6

A Flurry of Activity

The entire crew was assembled in the kitchen, all eyes on me and the double saddlebags resting on the tabletop.

"I take it we're moving right away," said Dandelion. "So far the only direct word we got from Hyrum was we were going to have some 'major changes'."

"All I know from my orders," said Rick Brazelton, "is to lay claim to enough wagons and stock to take us 200 miles—and that you would pay for the lot in hard cash."

I patted the saddlebags.

"What 'major changes' exactly is what I want to know," said Opal, adding her usual afterthought: "Only 'major changes' I'd like to see in Monterey is Reverend Cowan getting his arse tanned while Mrs. Cowan counts the strokes on her rosary beads."

"Opal!" scolded Dandelion.

"He don't say rosary beads," corrected Scarlet. "They're Presbyterians or something."

"What he is is distasteful to me from my earliest recollection of the man," said Mary Turtle-Eyes. "If he keeps poking his nose in our business I'm going to cut off my monthly tithe."

This brought a laugh, but, I found out much later, Mary Turtle-Eyes was known to toss a coin or two into a church poor box.

Scarlet, standing close to Rick Brazelton as if seeking his protection against the danger looming outside the Vista Del

Mar, spoke: "Cowan and his crowd want us out of Monterey. I reckon they are about to get their wish."

The next three weeks saw a flurry of activity at the Vista Del Mar. The wagons were paid for and delivered to the site. The mule-power gathered up in a corral. Brazelton and a pick-up group of day laborers began the deconstruction of the building one step behind the ladies inside gathering up their possessions and the interior fixtures. Because the kitchen was the first to be dismantled, young boys were hired to relay food for the crew from the eater at the foot of the hill. The Professor took charge of erecting temporary canvas quarters — one shelter per girl providing a modicum of privacy — the place of business might disappear from sight but not the business itself.

At six o'clock the work ceased, the workmen departed, and the young ladies began their work shift which was brisk since every sporting male from San José to San Luis Obispo knew the Vista Del Mar was closing down and fond good-byes were in order.

I had much to learn about females in general and prostitutes in particular. The Professor philosophized on the subject: "For two American dollars I could force any of our ladies to do every carnal passage their young bodies and my old one can imagine. That is the law under the Americans as it was under the Mexicans and also the Spaniards: value for value received. But, for a million dollars — American gold or Spanish silver, no matter which — you can not get one of these *muchachas* to walk outside without wearing a *pañuelo en la cabeza.*"[105]

One Sunday I found myself in Monterey with the opportunity to learn more about the Reverend Cowan. I slipped into his church and heard the following discourse which may have been directed at me: "A young man, impatient to slow growth and the legitimate exercise of

---

[105] Headscarf.

amativeness,[106] by example, or instinct bequeathed him by his parents, practices and delights in self-abuse...."[107]

His sermon continued more or less with these words: "...and without knowing of the fearful penalty in store for him, he continues it, until, as in thousands of cases, idiocy, insanity, or death sets in, and his parents or friends account for his ill health and premature death as being caused by consumption...

"These sad facts apply with equal force to the girls and young women among you, though not in the same ratio...."

All this was news to me. I looked about the congregation to see if his scathing pronouncement had caused visible discomfort to any of the girls or young women (there were very few of them in Monterey or, indeed, in all of Alta California) within earshot of the preacher.

"...how sadly must the high and holier part of a man's nature be lowered who can, without the smallest whisperings or conscience, enter the den of a professional prostitute!"

"Amen!" shouted a pock-marked matron in the front row. "Amen!" shouted back the congregation.

He at last had gotten to the subject of prostitution. Surely he knew he had won the day. Was this his victory oration? His salute to himself, the conqueror?

"...where are the thoughts, the feelings, the souls of such men?

"...Have they mothers loving and true?—sisters affectionate and pure?—wives confident and sincere? Apart from the degradation of soul, do such men know the risks they run? Do they know that every ninety-nine such women

---

[106] The facility supposed to influence sexual desire.

[107] The text of this sermon was indeed written by John Cowan—but not the John Cowan of Monterey. In 1869, J. S. Ogilvie published a book by John Cowan, M.D., *The Science of a New Life*. The connection between the two men is not clear, nor can we find a clue in C.H.'s notes. My conclusion—regrettably —is that C.H.'s portrayal of the John Cowan of Monterey is mostly fiction, C.H. probably sensing that a villain was needed to spice up his tale.

out of a hundred are diseased? — and that this dread disease, once in the system, is there forever; and if they have offspring their children's children even to four and five and even ten generations will be tainted."

He went on to describe in vivid detail the effects of syphilis — a "five year old boy with the roof of his mouth eaten away..." — which brought gasps to his congregation.

Then Rev. Cowan let fly in another direction: "There are women — strong, passionate and often diseased — who are endowed with strong animal natures, who, when they marry, in the intense exercise of their lustful natures, soon reduce the husband to a standard that physically and mentally places him below the brute." Furthermore: "The exercise of abnormal amativeness is known in all its intensity by those newly married. The honeymoon is one nightly repetition of legalized prostitution!"

At the conclusion of his dissertation, Rev. Cowan was frothing at the mouth. The angry red veins in his neck were standing like steel cords.

At this point in his frenzy, shared by his flock, he could have commanded the assemblage to walk into Monterey Bay to stop the very fishes from fornicating.[108]

Alas, the good minister had never harkened to Cicero who believed brevity to be a great praise of eloquence. Yet, I was amazed. How did he know all of these obsessions of humankind?

In any event, Dandelion reported business in the canvas shelters that evening topped even the receipts on the first Independence Day following the ratification of the Treaty of Guadalupe Hidalgo the year previous.[109]

---

[108] Which fish do not do. Hence the expression, "Poor fish."
[109] The treaty was ratified on February 2, 1848.

7

Reenter Billy Tremaine

Reenter Billy Tremaine. You will recall him in this narrative set in Nellie's Fleas—the "deckhand completing his first voyage." The sailor aboard the *Tronka* who "displayed uncommon courage when it came to climbing up to the crow's nest in the worst of horrible weather."

Billy Tremaine had kin in Monterey and it was to Monterey he emigrated immediately after a brass spittoon I was holding came to crack the skull of Second Mate Martin Bledsoe.

Billy's uncle, Phineas Tremaine, was on his way to becoming a millionaire, thanks to the Gold Rush. He ran a dry goods / hardware warehouse in Monterey, stocking it with manufactured goods purchased from the occasional merchantman which mistook Monterey Bay for San Francisco Bay. A pick-and-shovel combination for which Phineas paid a dollar, a dozen for ten dollars, sold for ten dollars at one of Phineas's Stockton, Placerville or Sacramento canvas stores.

I had much business to transact with Phineas. I quickly learned that he was the embodiment of the term, "Yankee Trader." It means sharp, shrewd, crafty, clever, cunning, canny—take your pick, or choose all of them. One had to keep one's wits about him when doing business with Phineas Tremaine.

Billy had a bit of the Yankee Trader in him. He had made the round trip to Stockton for his uncle, and took an interest in my enterprise by way of searching out some angle from which he could profit.

The truth will out: Billy was seeking an assignment that would cause him to be absent from Monterey for weeks and even months. It had nothing to do with what Billy had done — it concerned what Uncle Phineas and Aunt Ruth had in mind to do to Billy: marry him off to Rev. John and Abigail[110] Cowan's daughter Hope — shy, homely, frightened-to-death-of-everything animate and inanimate.

The Billy Tremaine comic-tragedy was playing out on our little stage. He made frequent trips to the Vista Del Mar site, delivering bags of nails and tweaks of snuff shorted on the previous delivery.

Every visit caught Billy the pawn descending deeper and deeper in a downward spiral leading to matrimony: Uncle Phineas and Aunt Ruth reasoned that the Tremaine-Cowan union would insure their place at the top of the Mid-California social scene, such as it was.

If Phineas was concerned about Billy's frequent and longer in duration visits to the Vista Del Mar deconstruction site, he made no inclination of such. We were Tremaine Hardware's best and always-ready-with-cash customer. Money took precedence over morality with Phineas. Sure, he was doing business with a notorious whorehouse, but he was participating in the removal of that quagmire of sin. Rarely, reasoned Phineas, was one able to do God's work *and* turn a profit.

During this time a problem I knew I would eventually have to deal with made itself known. Rick Berazelton asked me if I knew one Zachary Fenner who was "poking around asking questions."

"He's looking to dig up some dirt on Hyrum Milton," I said.

---

[110] Abigail Cowan outlived everyone in this narrative. She was 111 years old when she died. After John Cowan died, she married a Swiss dairyman named Fritz Werner, and they settled in Soledad south of Salinas.

At our 6 o'clock "meeting" that evening I reiterated the warning, explaining that Hyrum, so far as I could tell, had some political ambitions that would be ruined by a Vista Del Mar scandal.

"What's this crow look like?" asked Dandelion. Brazelton gave a description and I added to it.

"Is he the sporting kind?" Daphne asked.

"I doubt it," Brazelton answered.

"I don't know a man alive who isn't the sporting kind when you give him a close look at Madam Pussy," said Opal.

For once, Dandelion did not upbraid Opal. "Next time he shows up let's kick his arse," she said.

"That'll bring the Monterey Constabulary down on us," I said.

Opal, with her usual: "I've screwed every member of the constabulary...."

Princess: "Most of them have gone to the diggings...."

Scarlet, to Opal: "Was it your screwing or the placer gold out there that caused them to skip out?"

Opal sprang to her feet instantaneously followed by Dandelion. "Calm down, all of you," she commanded.

Rick Brazelton, who never before to my knowledge had interjected himself in the "personnel" side of the enterprise, attempted to quell the flare up by assuring Opal that Scarlet meant no harm in her comment, and, further: "We've always got to keep in mind who are friends are and who our friends ain't."

Daphne had a question: "What's the to do on the hardware merchant's son? I heard him called 'Billy'."

Opal, still in a stew, gave a tart answer to Daphne: "You know damned well his name is Billy and he's old man Tremaine's nephew, not his son."

Rick Brazelton: "Word's out he's going to marry Cowan's daughter, Hope."

This caused the girls variously to grunt, laugh, gasp, cry

out....

"Skinny-assed Hope?" Opal asked. "The pimpled-faced Cowan girl we'd see on the road to the mushroom pickings?"

I took the floor. "I think Billy has a problem that we might be able to fix," I said. "He's taken the Stockton road a couple of times and we could use him as a guide. More important, we need another teamster.

"So how do we fix his problem?" asked Daphne, who appeared to be the most interested in Billy's fate.

"We give him some breathing room," I answered.

"And what are the uncle and Cowan going to think about darling Billy being in the whorehouse moving business?" asked Gertie.

I gave this explanation: "The uncle will only concern himself with the wages Billy will earn—and split 50-50 with the uncle—from the transport and re-assembly of Vista Del Monte. With Billy on the scene, all of our hardware business will settle on the Tremaine store in Stockton.

"So far as Cowan is concerned, Billy will be doing God's work by removing the whorehouse from the Monterey diocese. And I suspect Hope might need a bit more convincing before she is ready to trade mushroom picking for the embarrassing ordeal of having the male member inserted into her belly."

With this I asked for a democratic vote as to whether or not I would approach my old shipmate with a job offer. All were in favor except Daphne.

Billy was more than amenable to the scheme. Now I had to sell it to his uncle, which proved no more difficult than counting the legs on a three-legged stool. "Of course Billy can take on this work, but your wages seem a mite low," Phineas said trying to get his face to smile.

"That's the number I'm bound to hold," I answered—and then from out the corner of the cluttered room came a voice I recognized: "Bound to hold by whose orders?"

It was Zachary Fenner at his spy work.

"Mr. Tremaine has your answer in his tally sheets," I said. Then to Tremaine: "Show him the entries — it's all written down."

"There is no name associated with our dealings," Phineas Tremaine said.

"His name is certain writ down," I said. " — see, here it is — 'Mr. Cash'."

When all was settled and Billy took up his work chiefly loading the wagons with the bones of the Vista Del Mar, he was heard to say, "Does a man good to leave the smoke of his own chimney."

8

On Bayard Taylor

Here I must digress to pick up another strand of my adventure in Monterey: the matter of Bayard Taylor.

He was in the thick of the Constitutional Convention, recognized by everyone on the Monterey streets as an important New York writer. By the same token I too had universal recognition: the young man who is dismantling the whorehouse at the crest of the road leading to Mission Carmel.

It was important that I not compromise Bayard by publically acknowledging our acquaintanceship, so the first time we met eye-to-eye no iota of recognition passed between us. The same the next time and the time after that. Finally, we positioned ourselves so that I could deliver a clandestine message: "I'm camped in a tent near our corral at the base of bald tree which I will mark with a flag."

"What sort of flag?" Bayard asked.

"My red BVDees."[111]

He arrived at my tent carrying a blanket. It seems the cuartel was overrun with fleas. "There was one subject," he said, "that dominated all conversation at the Presidio. Fleas are annoyance by no means peculiar to California, they haunt the temples of the Incas and the halls of the Montezumas; I have felt them come upon me in the Pantheon of Rome, and many a traveler has bewailed their visitation while sleeping in the shadow of the Pyramids.

---

[111] Not hardly. The New York firm of Bradley, Voorhees, and Day created the flannel underwear in 1878.

"Nothing is more positively real to the feelings, nothing more elusive and intangible to the search. You look upon the point of their attack, and you see it not; you put your finger on it, and it is not there.

"We tried all means in our power to procure a good night's rest. We swept out the room, shook out the blankets, tucked ourselves in so skillfully that we thought no flea could effect an entrance. But in vain.

"At last, after a week of waking torment, I determined to give up the attempt; I had become so nervous by repeated failures that the thought of it alone would have prevented sleep."[112]

Bayard liked my "hotel" — especially the sweet scented air found here away from the shoreline.

"Why is it the Vista Del Mar's uncommonly high number of beds does not suffer from the flea?" I asked my guest. "What uncommon odor do you detect in the breezes playing about us?"

"It smells of the forest," said Bayard.

"Exactly," I said, "and so does the interior of the Vista Del Mar. There is a thick green shrub growing hereabouts which our learned major-domo, one Pablo Perez, regularly harvests and regularly stuffs in the attic — a thick green shrub whose powerful balsamic odor is too much for the fleas, but not too much for the understandably preoccupied patrons of our humble digs."

"Balsam!" cried Bayard. "The breath of angels."[113]

"And that breath extends to this tent. We are surrounded with a *chevaux-de-frise* of balsam." My declaration directed the conversation to the Convention: "Tell me about the fate of California. Why does Fremont look so haggard? Will Sutter's crony, Barnett, be our first civilian governor? Will the Tennessee man, Gwinn, talk the convention to death?"

---

[112] This discourse on the flea is lifted entirely from Bayard's *El Dorado*.
[113] Actually, there is no balsam plant per se. Balsam is the resinous exudate (sap) of several plants — "The balm of Gilead."

"Hold on," said Bayard. "You have more inside stuffing than I do. Who are your spies?"

"The girls," I answered. "Your delegates and their clerks visit them more to grab a sympathetic ear than they do to grab other parts of the anatomy that might prove more interesting."

From Bayard I learned the major political problem facing California was not the suitability or unsuitability of the document then being drafted in Monterey; it was, instead, the attitude Federal congressmen—North and South—would have regarding the "upstart" Westerners.

"After all," he pointed out, "half of your population resides in the southern half of California—people who only a few months back had taken up arms against the United States, and the other half peopled by irregulars, drifters, fortune-seekers, and misfits.

"This is a strange convention," Bayard said. "Riley[114] assumed over much in convening it. Congress will balk. The delegates are young[115] and inexperienced in matters of statecraft."

The Southern Californians would rather be separate from the North, Bayard observed. Territorial[116] status would be more to their liking. And there is the general attitude of the delegates toward the United States: "If they don't do this or if

---

[114] Brigadier General Bennett Riley, veteran of the War of 1812, the Black Hawk and Mexican wars, had arrived in mid-April to take over the civil government of California from Col. Mason. Riley was a "grim old fellow and a fine free swearer," and when he learned Congress had adjourned without arriving at a solution as to whether the conquered Mexican territory should be slave or free he took it upon himself to let the people decide. ¶ Riley issued a call for a constitutional convention in Monterey, asking that delegates be elected in August from 10 districts: San Diego, Santa Barbara, San Luis Obispo, Los Angeles, Sonoma, Sacramento, San Joaquin, Monterey, San José, and San Francisco. In all there were 48 delegates. A dozen of that number were gold-rushers newly arrived in California. The others were *Californios*—Vallejo, De la Guerra, Carrillo; some were Americans of long residency—Stearns, Larkin; four, including John Sutter, had been born out of the country.

[115] Nine of the delegates were under 30; 23 were under 40.

they don't do that, then, by God, we'll make our own nation out here. The 'Republic of the Pacific' I think they call it."

And on what matter, pray, have the delegates spent most of their time and energy? What theme of urgency concerning the welfare—nay, the very existence—of California? What topic brings forth the most splendid oratory, the most succulent rhetoric, a veritable cascade of metaphors, similes and images?

Whether California should permit or ban dueling.

"And slavery," I asked. "Won't that be the cause for a few carelessly-hurled words?"

"It will never get started at this convention," said Bayard. "Many of these men are from Southern states, but all have been exposed to this new free-flowing society, and they rather like it. Slavery will be prohibited in California and the delegates will vote unanimously on that issue."

Bayard made his point: "Slavery means living among Negroes. The Northerners are hypocrites on that score. The reason they are against slavery is not because they cannot bear to see men in chains; they simply want no Negroes in California."

"Well then tell me about Fremont and his long face," I said.

"Fremont wants to be your first Senator," said Bayard. "What upsets him is money. Before he went East, he turned his life's worth to Larkin[117] with instructions to buy a certain ranch worthy of a U.S. Senator. Instead, Larkin bought a 70-square-mile plot of worthless rock called the Mariposa,[118] a hundred miles from nowhere."

---

[116] California skipped that step, went directly from "republic" to statehood.

[117] Thomas O. Larkin was the first and only consul to Mexican Alta California.

[118] Of course the Mariposa was fabulously wealthy. The first gold from its mines reached Fremont in Monterey about the time C.H. relates this passage. But, the Mariposa proved to be Fremont's financial undoing. He was never able to gain free title to the land, a former Spanish grant. He faced poverty in his declining years.

9

Trapping Zachary Fenner

Billy Tremaine's work was of profound and abiding interest to his aunt, Ruth. Perhaps the cheap romances she read accounted for a latent desire she had to be ravaged by a pirate crew. Her barren marriage to Phineas Tremaine had only resulted in numbers on a bank statement—numbers that Phineas would never exchange for an elegant Tiffany[119] table lamp with a ruby dragonfly motif.

Auntie Ruth could not mask her curiosity. "Do the women carry on in the open? She asked.

"Carry on what?" Billy teased.

"You know," said Ruth.

"I wouldn't know. I've never seen the women in their tents," Billy said. "Besides, there's a whole mess of work to be done tearing down and packing that place. I haven't got time to go about sneaking." This was, of course, an exaggeration which Billy hoped would throw the old lady off the scent.

The truth is Billy usually ate his lunch with Daphne. Although the conversation usually had to do with some aspect of clothing and fashion, he noticed it was having some effect on him. He took time in the morning to make sure his garb was free of grime and otherwise presentable. Daphne was known to turn down a "client" who presented himself in soiled clothing. This bit of intelligence he did not share with Aunt Ruth.

[119] Charles Lewis Tiffany and John Young started the luxury glass and jewelry works in New York City in 1837. Tiffany's only sold for cash, and each items was clearly marked as to its price to forestall haggling. Phineas would not have enjoyed shopping at Tiffany's.

Although Billy was "doing God's work" by tearing down the Vista Del Mar, Rev. Cowan did not want it known that his probable future son-in-law was consorting with the deviants on the high road to Carmel.

From time to time when Billy returned home after work, Hope Cowan would be at the Tremaine home. She usually had little to say by way of topical conversation, but on one occasion she blurted out, "How'd you contract for this job, Billy?" Her feminine instincts, though barely developed, told her that their impending separation would not work to her benefit.

Mrs. Cowan, who happened to be at the Tremaine home on that evening, gave a sharp reprimand to her daughter: "Hope! Trouble yourself with your knitting."

Auntie Ruth would have none of it. "Now, Abigail," she said, "Hope has every right to know Billy's doings...."

Billy made a mental comment: "Shit! That does it. We're engaged!"

Billy was not privy to the Hyrum Milton connection to our curious enterprise, and a good thing. He was prone to gossiping. Indeed, we knew more about the habits of the Cowan and Tremaine families that we needed or wished to know. And he filled us in on the idiosyncrasies of Zackary Fenner, who spent an inordinate amount of time going through the incoming mail, volunteering his help in sorting the letters for the under-worked postmaster, Benjamin Conn.

The post-office had two windows. Conn would spend the entire day hunkering down in one window, supporting his massive head on his elbows, while his helper, Daniel Longworth did all the work. A person wishing to buy a stamp would place his order with Conn who would then bellow to his helper, Daniel Longworth, at that moment struggling with some mail sacks in the back of the building, to drop what he was doing and come to the front to service the customer, "With a little speed, please."

Billy did not spare us the bad news. I rather think he

relished telling it, probably something to do with him being a lowly deck hand and me a paying passenger aboard the Tronka. "They're going about town calling you the 'Pimp Man,'" Billy reported. "This Zachary Fenner muck-raker got up on his hind legs in the Bible Class and asked if anyone had the dirt on you. One farmer told that before you came his berry patch made more than he could eat and now he can't pick enough berries in a day to satisfy his appetite." According to Billy's Bible Class informants, several others reported damnable actions on my part, even holding my presence in Monterey responsible for the flea infestation.

"Next time you meet with these folks, Billy, I suggest you get them to study the Ninth Commandment,"[120] I said.

Meanwhile, Zachary Fenner stepped up his efforts. He tracked down the two blacks I rode in on, and copied their brands.[121] He singled out arrival from San Francisco for possible intelligence regarding the political scene—a name might pop up.

But his most egregious act—the one that cooked his goose—came about thusly:

Bayard made frequent "flea runs" to my flea-free balsamic Eden (minus—I must vehemently point out—an Eve). There I caught up with the latest news regarding the birth-pangs of a State, and I, in turn, filled in Bayard on the progress being made in preparation for our forthcoming Exodus. When the subject of Zachary Fenner came up Bayard voiced his surprise in seeing Delegate Fenner sorting through the mail in the open window next to our esteemed postmaster, Benjamin Conn.

We set a trap.

---

[120] Thou shalt not bear false witness against thy neighbor.

[121] Branding livestock has been around for thousands of years. There is Biblical evidence that Jacob, the great herdsman, branded his stock. But, if Zachary Fenner is indeed hoping to uncover the name of the mystery Vista Del Mar owner by way of tracing original ownership via brands on the two black horses, he is wasting his time—unless his patrons are paying him by the hour. It was not until 1917 that California enacted the Hide and Brand Law, thus creating a brand design registry.

We wrote a letter, addressed "confidential" to me, showing no name of the sender, with this message: "I will be in Monterey incognito on the 12th. Meet me 9 p.m. at the crossroads below the Presidio. I will bring letters of credit for you to sign. I appreciate your good work." — unsigned

Bayard asked Lieutenants James Whiteside[122] and Martin Hayes[123] to assist in what appeared to be a case of mail fraud — a serious Federal offense — occurring under the proud military's collective noses. He filled them in on the details. Both officers knew Fenner, of course, and were not surprised that he was a suspect.

A full hour before the appointed time, Bayard and I were at the lean-to shelter at the crossroads while the two officers stood hidden in the roadside foliage with orders (actually suggestions) that they arrest the first person to reconnoiter the trysting place.

And, true to form, that person was a very rattled Zachary Fenner who could only have known where and when I was to meet with my employer by having illegally read the letter intended "confidentially" for me.

And, lo!!! He had with him the slothful Postmaster Benjamin Conn!!!

The two lieutenants, having cleared their participation with their superiors, came armed not only with their Colt .36 caliber Navy Revolvers[124] but with drawn sabers as well.

The officers explained the situation at hand. Because of the Army's desire not to besmirch the workings of the Convention with a postal scandal, Fenner was given 24 hours to resign as a delegate and leave the Convention. He was to have no contact

---

[122] Whiteside died at age 40 from eating poison alpha-amanitin mushrooms, aka Destroying Angel.

[123] Hayes remained in the Army, rising in rank to Colonel when he was killed in the First Battle of Bull Run (First Manassas) on July 21, 1861.

[124] C.H. may be guessing here. The Colt .36 came into use by the military in 1851. Before that was the much heavier 1847 Colt .44 Dragoon. No matter, Zachary was duly impressed.

with the Vista Del Mar operation upon disclosure in the sealed indictment of Fenner's *prima facie* felony.

Postmaster Conn, for having received bribes from Fenner, and thus betraying his trust, was to leave Monterey immediately after he had turned in his keys — which meant that very night for the military men were determined to march Conn over to the home of Daniel Longworth, by virtue invested by a pair of Colt .36 caliber Navy Revolvers, for the transfer of postal power and padlock keys to said Daniel Longworth.

The sudden departure of Fenner/Conn left the Reverend John Cowan in an agitated state of curiosity not knowing the why of the matter, and in an equally agitated state of depression, he having lost two staunch allies in his eternal struggle against Satan.

The Army had a hand in this, but one does not sermonize against a conquering Army. The one certainty was that the victory went to the Vista Del Mar according to Billy Tremaine's description of the goings-on in the compound the day after the Fenner/Conn exile became known.

At first, Rev. Cowan thought of going directly to the commanding officer at the Presidio and ask....

No, that wouldn't do. Cowan wasn't sure what specifically he needed to ask....

He didn't have to. Our two lieutenants paid a visit to Rev. Cowan. After the preliminary "we want to apprise you as a leader in this community as to what has transpired with Mr. Fenner and Mr. Cobb," they gave a one-sentence explanation:

"These two gentlemen were engaged in a mail fraud scheme the particulars of which we have sealed on condition that they do not return to Monterey."

"And the Vista Del Mar?" asked Rev. Cowan.

The lieutenants (they told Bayard) acted surprise, answering, "We know nothing of the Vista Del Mar or what it might have to do with the Fenner/Cobb matter." Case closed — perhaps. There is always a perhaps....

10

Finishing Up in Monterey

Genius must conceive, but patient labor must consummate.

Our work of demolition of the storied Chinese box of pleasure was complete, the pieces neatly secured on a half-dozen wagons. Our fleet featured a 12-person wagonette carriage, the two seating benches facing one another. Only the wagonette had springs. This vehicle the ladies and their luggage would call home for, hopefully, only at most two weeks.

There were two hay wagons—monstrous trucks with hind wheels six-feet high. Twenty feet above the ground the driver would perch, not so much concerned with mud and ruts on the roadway as he will be with low-lying oak[125] branches.

The three buckboards were common to every "farm" in California. But, uncommon was the bright yellow the Professor chose to paint them. And because Phineas Tremaine not only had the only supply of paint—a barrel of bright yellow—he refused to sell a portion of it: "Here's how it came and here's how it goes—the whole barrel or let your wagons blister and peel in the San Joaquin." The two hay wagons and the wagonette received the same bright yellow treatment.

"Can we head out at night?" Dandelion asked. "The ladies don't much cotton to being part of a circus parade."

"To hell with that," said Opal. "I'm for going right down

---

[125] The miners called the oak tree a "widow maker" for the propensity of its large limbs to snap off. No veteran gold seeker made his bed under an oak branch.

Lighthouse Avenue at high noon and calling out the names of all our customers—'Hey, Louie, how's the wife?' 'Mr. Peck, you forgot your hat.' 'Delegate Humphrey, I'm going to miss your big Charlie!'"

After the laughter died down, a somber veneer descended over the room. The ladies knew they would never be able to hold a mirror to the Good Citizens so they could see their cruel and hurtful hypocrisy.

During the month or so it took us to tear down the Vista Del Mar, there was a noticeable decline in the number of locals out and about. As it was with every settlement in Alta California, the diggings were draining off their men, and the hordes that arrived by sea did not stop even briefly at the towns but headed directly to the Sierra Nevada foothills.

San Francisco far eclipsed Monterey as a port of entry, but an occasional clipper ship[126] put into the bay here. A few of these emigrants visited the Vista Del Mar, but, according to the girls, they seemed "preoccupied" by visions of gold.

Word got out via Billy that Daphne was outscoring her sisters in the parlor line-ups by a hefty margin, until it was surmised that the reason for her success was a heavy gold chain she wore around her neck. That was only a working thesis, but plausible: *Gemmis auroque teguntur omnia; par minima est ipsa puella sui.*[127]

Gold fever had not as yet affected us. The Professor had been to the mines and had returned unscathed. Billy made a few trips to Stockton and had returned unscathed. Rick had gone to Sonoran Camp to stake out a site for the Vista Del Monte and had returned unscathed.

---

[126] The clipper ship was a fast yacht-like vessel built for speed. It was narrow and carried three masts and a square rig. Its boom years began in 1843 to fulfill the British market for China tea. The California Gold Rush provided further impetus, but it all ended for the clipper ship in 1869 with the opening of the Suez Canal.

[127] "Jewels and gold cover everything; very little of our love is for the girl herself." A quote from Ovid.

Who else? Scarlet and Princess came to the Vista Del Mar as a duo, having met and briefly "worked" Placerville. They gave it up and headed for San Francisco, but they were on the wrong stage and after four or five transfers ended up in Monterey.

The Professor changed our mind set concerning gold. One day at Phineas Tremaine's he ran into, literally, a cousin—a very drunk cousin returning from the mines on his way home to Hermosillo. But this cousin staggered not from alcohol but from the weight of the gold he had distributed on every quadrant of his body. Convincing his kin that the Professor was associated with honorable folk ("No whore I ever knew was 'honorable'," the cousin observed) and they would show him how to get his gold home safe and sound.

The key to this would be a letter of credit (from the French *"accreditivus"* which means "the power to do something). And the key to the key was to solicit the advice of Thomas O. Larkin,[128] the United States's first and only consul to Mexican California. Larkin was in Monterey attending the convention. With Fenner no longer snooping around the village we felt it safe to meet publically and it was at one such gathering—Larkin, Bayard, Rick, me, the Professor, and the gold-bearer Hernando Perez who could hardly bend to sit in a chair so constricted was he by his literal and figurative *camisa de fuerza*.[129]

Larkin explained to Cousin Hernando that a letter of credit from the U.S. Army to the American Army ligation in Hermosillo would be far safer than dodging the Mexican *banditos* in the state of Sonora.

"How much it cost?" Hernando asked.

"Three per cent," answered Larkin.

Hernando gave his cousin a scathing look, pupil-to-pupil. As he struggled to stand he said, "If I don't get my gold in

---

[128] See footnote 117.
[129] Straightjacket.

Hermosillo, Pablo, I will send you a letter of credit containing your mother's eyes."[130]

At the Presidio weighing of Hernando's treasure, I was struck not only by the volume of gold he disgorged, but at its beauty, especially those pieces embedded in quartz. In the words of a New Hampshire man I would meet later in Sonoran Camp, "A frenzy seized my soul when I picked up my first nugget."

I was, of course, familiar with gold, but never had I seen it heaped up so on the scale. My sleeping tent was too small to hold my imagination—I saw piles of gold rising before me at every step...castles of marble...servants dressing me in satins...rich custard tarts—and Burgundia.

As we neared the end of the Monterey phase of our operation, the ladies had a great deal to say about their clientele.

"All the able-bodied are off digging for gold," said Gertie. Opal, of course, had something to add to the conversation: "Every time a cricket farts, some of those old fools leap about like whalers coming off of a three-year arse-less cruise."

"I've been working in the dark," put in Daphne. "Some of the men left in this town are so ugly, it's better in the dark."

"Don't they complain about it being dark?" asked Opal. "Hell's fire, most of them coots want it blazing sunlight so they can get their money's worth. 'Come over here handsome, and take a long hard look at this pretty fur piece'."

"Opal!" It was Gertie, the emotional one, who admonished her sister. "We all know what we are and what we do, but why do you insist in rubbing our noses in it?"

"What we are and what we do—is that so damned wrong?" replied the outspoken Opal. "At least we don't sneak around behind a respectful apron swishing our pussies at the lonely neighbor rancher or the well-hung butcher-shop delivery boy."

---

[130] So far as I know, Hernando Perez collected his money.

"Opal! Opal!" This time it was Mary Turtle-Eyes. "We do what we do for money. It is a business. A hard business. A sinful business. We will burn in hell for what we do. In order to keep our sanity we must dwell on the positive. Ours is an ancient calling. We are consorts. We give pleasure. We give what God in his wisdom gave us the ability to give with art and beauty."

"Listen," said Opal, not about to be lectured into a corner, "The old-cocks I consort with in this town want no art or beauty. They want someone underneath them who will gallop when they want to gallop; canter when they want to canter; and trot when they want to trot. That's fine with me. The only ones who bother me are the coots who want to walk their horses all the way across the pasture and into the barn."

The comment brought forth no rejoinder. Finally, Mary Turtle-Eyes smoothed the gown covering her shapely bosom, and said: "We love you, Opal."

The other young ladies sealed Mary's pronouncement with broad smile.

Expecting bloodshed, I had witnessed instead the strewing of rose petals along a very hard road. To myself I wondered: "Who can fathom the manner in which women reason and reach conclusions?"

11

John C. Fremont

Our attention now turns briefly to John C. Fremont, who had invited the Constitution delegates and the rest of the Monterey populace to an open-house reception.

Bayard brought the news.

"I'm sure," I told him, "that Fremont's broad invitation is not broad enough to include whorehouse movers."

"Nonsense," said Bayard. "It's an open house and you are a significant force for good in Monterey. Of course, if you were erecting instead of demolishing a whorehouse, it would be a different story.

"All hail Caesar Honore, public benefactor!"

"What purpose would it serve me or the public to take tea with the Fremonts?" I asked.

"The purpose of seeing history close up," Bayard answered. "When you are an old man you can tell your grandchildren that once way back in 1849 you met the 'Pathfinder.'"

"I don't want to tell them that my presence incited a riot, topped off by a Holy War," I said.

"There will be no riot," Bayard said.

"There will be if the Rev. Cowan is there to lead us—at least 'some of us'—in prayer."

"History," said Bayard, "will not remember the Cowans. Oh, perhaps he will lend his name to a Monterey alley-way; but history will remember the Fremonts.[131]

"The Cowans of this world are clever sorts who know the knack of climbing aboard the leaves being swept forward by the winds of events. The Fremonts are those winds."

"And the Taylors?" I asked. "Surely your writings will endure."[132]

"I am hardly a 'Pathfinder'," said my friend. "When we rode together to Monterey I confess it crossed my mind that our association might not be the best thing to forward my professional career, but I never doubted it would do wonders for my personal career."

"I appreciate those words," I said. "But, I see no benefit to either of us or, for that matter, the Fremonts, if I should go to their tea party and constantly pointed to as a 'California Rarity'."

---

[131] C.H. gives us a great deal of detail regarding John Charles and Jessie Benton Fremont, and I do not wish to overburden the reader with more on the Fremonts than is necessary. However, we should remind ourselves that the stuff the Fremonts were made of is the very stuff that gives America her strength.¶ In the 1870's, when the Fremonts suffered financial loss after being on the very pinnacle of success, Mrs. Fremont began to contribute regularly to periodicals, and some of her stories appeared in volume form. *Far West Sketches* was published in 1890. ¶ Fremont's tragedy is that he strayed from exploration of the West onto fields in which he was a babe in the woods. His impulses were essentially kinetic. He was rash and lacked practical judgment—but when we stack up his accomplishments against his mistakes, we find that truly this was a great man of California and the West. ¶ Their daughter, Elizabeth Benton Fremont, wrote lovingly of her parents. Some examples: "My mother's knowledge of Spanish was a great help to her in those days of travel in Central America and California, proving the wisdom of my grandfather (Senator Benton), when he had her learn the 'neighbor language' as he termed it, 'that she might talk over the back fence without the fear of the trouble that an interpreter might easily ferment.'" ¶ Mother worked hard as did father for the admission of California as a free state...there was strong pressure on father in an effort to induce him to lend his influence toward bringing California in as a slave state. It was pointed out that slave labor would make him a millionaire on his mining estate...many a vote was won by a sight of mother, a delicate young Southern woman, cheerfully doing her own work rather than take any steps that might influence the adoption of slavery into our splendid territory...my mother was by birth and tradition opposed to slavery...my father believed in those days that California was a paradise of free labor, an opinion that never changed to the end of his days."

[132] See footnotes 54 and 84.

"When we rode together to Monterey it crossed my mind that you may have been an impediment to my standing as an impartial reporter of the California scene," Bayard said. "But, I was looking at the situation through Eastern and not California eyes."

"Meaning what?" I asked.

"Meaning that I did not at first appreciate what you and thousands of other California Argonauts represent."

"Which is?"

"The spirit of 'live and let live.' A sort of tolerance...."

"A damned poor sort of tolerance," I said. "The Mexican and Chilean miners are hardly tolerated."[133]

"California is a new world," Bayard continued. "Fremont will welcome into his home the men writing a constitution for that new world—and he'll welcome the men who work with their hands and those who work with their brains and those who write about the new world and the young man from Boston charged with relocating a whorehouse, the young man who stood up to the church hypocrite, the young man who was honorable in his business dealings...."

"Is everything about me common knowledge?" I asked.

"Your young ladies, I understand, are exceptional conversationalists. Do you think they can pass the opportunity to romanticize events that preoccupy their hours?"

"I defer to your judgment, Bayard," I said. "I shall accompany you to Fremont's tea party. After all, you have far more to lose than I."

"Neither of us will lose," said Bayard. "On the contrary, we shall tip a teacup with Fremont and that could be the single most important encounter in either of our lives.[134] He could be President.[135] He could order a conquest and

---

[133] In 1850 the new California Legislature imposed a $20 per month tax on "foreign miners," i.e. Latin Americans. Non-English speaking Europeans generally were exempt from the tax. The next year the tax was repealed primarily because of pressure from merchants whose businesses suffered from the sharp decrease in trade with the Latinos.

colonization of Canada, Mexico and South America. Because he believes in the West, our grandchildren may someday awaken the Chinese Sleeping Dragon to a duel for mastery of the world. Fremont is important for he has wild and still fluid visions of a new world."

The Fremont party took place on a balmy evening filled with the light of stars and the song of crickets. The house[136] they were renting was by far the most beautiful in Monterey, if not the whole of California. It was, in fact, the home of Jose Castro, late Mexican military *comandante*. Further, the Fremonts rented but half of the huge house, the self-exiled Castro's wife and children making up the other half of this incongruous household.

The thick adobe walls were a brilliant whitewash, and the red-tiled roof slanted over a spacious set of rooms and large open-air patios. These areas were paved with yellow and green tiles. Hanging from the eaves were *ollas* overflowing

---

[134] Actually C.H. met many men at least or more "important" than Fremont, including, as previously stated, Webster. He met Grant, whom he characterized as "thick." As a delegate to the Democratic National Conventions from 1872 to 1912, he had occasion to meet many important men. Grover Cleveland he regarded as "great." One of his last letters was to Woodrow Wilson, pledging his support at the convention of 1912 that eventually nominated him. C.H. said the greatest man he ever met was an illiterate Eskimo who "possessed the wisdom of all ages." The Eskimo, Baru-Tok by name, had, in C. H.'s words, "discovered the key to the good life: maintain healthy bowels." C.H. spent the summer of 1900 in Alaska on family business.

[135] Actually, he could not be President. Nominated for that office by the anti-slavery Republican Party in 1856, he lost the election to James B. Buchanan, a Democrat. He was elected (by the Legislature) California Senator on September 9, 1850, and Fremont was appointed Territorial Governor of Arizona (1878-81) by Rutherford B. Hayes.

[136] As described by Elizabeth Benton Fremont, the house was a "fine old adobe built in the usual fashion, around three sides of a court, which made a fine playground for Modesta Castro and myself...[the house had] long adobe rooms made cheerful and bright by the fire...the comfortable cane chairs recently imported from Canton China. I played on the furs that were liberally spread on the uncarpeted floor...."

with geraniums whose red colors danced in the light of torches and *luminarios*. A hedge of pink Roses of Castile marked the boundary between house and Monterey.

Fremont was not in military uniform, of course, having recently suffered the humiliation of his court-martial, but there were many uniforms in the great salon leaving one to believe the Army's fight with the Pathfinder had been more routine than rigorous.[137]

Fremont, unfortunate in his illegitimate birth, poverty, and undisciplined early schooling, was fortunate in his scientific training and especially in his marriage. To some he was forever the brilliant amateur, but in reality he was an expert topographer and careful observer. One need only contrast his work to that of Meriwether Lewis and William Clark who led a band of simple soldiers and frontiersmen. Fremont led hardworking, meticulous survey crews into that same Western wilderness.

His tragedy had roots in his propensity to stray from his scientific career—into politics, into business, into military power plays.

Jessie Fremont stood at the Pathfinder's side. She was the highborn daughter of Senator Thomas Benton,[138] the most powerful man—including the President—in Washington City, and as such had had a lifetime's dealings with the most refined stratum of society, of which California was understandably

---

[137] The verdict against him did him no harm. Public opinion was solidly on Fremont's side. During the Mexican-American War, Commodore Robert Stockton appointed Fremont military governor of California. When General Stephen Kearny, who outranked Stockton, asked Fremont to give up the governorship, Fremont stubbornly refused. For disobeying a direct order from a superior office, Fremont was court-martialed, found guilty, and dismissed from the service. However, President Polk commuted the sentence. When Kearny, on his death bed in St. Louis, learned that Mrs. Fremont was in town, asked to see her, she refused, blaming him for the stress she suffered during the time of the court-martial, resulting in the loss of a child she was carrying.

[138] Senator Benton was the Democratic floor leader of the Senate, the leading proponent of Western expansion. He was pompous, vain, and

lacking.

I liked Jessie Fremont immediately, for she greeted with the same restrained cordiality that was used on all else in the line that stretched before and after me.

Certainly she knew who I was, and so did Fremont. I caught a corner of their mouths in a shared smile.

"My house is your house," said Fremont, using the familiar Spanish greeting.

"Not quite," I said, hurriedly giving way to Bayard to facilitate my escape. "Colonel Fremont, Mrs. Fremont," said my companion, "you have chosen a beautiful evening for this reception."

Fremont replied: "I trust you come as a friend on pleasure rather than a journeyman to work."

"I come as both," replied Bayard. "The latter must feed and clothe the former."

"I don't know about clothing you, Bayard," said Jessie Fremont, "but of food and drink there is aplenty here. And as I know how miserably the *Herald* pays even its most celebrated writer, you are welcome to stop by our kitchen on your way home to make yourself a package of whatever provisions remain."[139]

Standing next in line after Bayard was an obese *Californio* hugely smiling at the friendly exchange between Jessie Fremont and Bayard, and when his turn came, he received a like ration.

I believe the entire permanent and temporary population of Monterey, save the Vista Del Mar crew, was in attendance. And, of course the Reverend John Cowan was positioned as far from the wine bar as the adobe walls would allow.

---

arrogant, but in this stormy age of our nation, he represented the view of middle America.

[139] Mrs. Fremont was genuine in her liking of literary people. She herself, as mentioned previously, was to become a successful writer and she was responsible for the editing of much of her husband's popular histories of his Western explorations. It was Jessie Fremont who gave Bret Harte encouragement and entrée to Eastern publishers.

12

Doc and Phiggy

We had six wagons and four drivers. I was not keen to take aboard any two of the day laborers we had working at the Vista del Mar, and none of them seemed keen on participating in an adventure.

I discussed this problem with Bayard one evening at the Balsam Arms and he had a ready solution.

"Your two drivers are ready, willing, and able to take on your task," he said. "At present they reside at the Presidio...."

"At the Presidio?"

"In the brig."

And so it was that the United States Army paroled to me two gentlemen of the first rank.

Let us take them one at a time:

Milford Brewer, native of Connecticut, 36 years of age, a self-styled "doctor" of phrenology, physiognomy, and human nature who flim-flammed his way into the Army by passing himself off as a real doctor of medicine and who famously extracted an Indian arrow in a man's buttocks by gently causing the missile to continue on its intended course. For this he gained much renown—from which the publicity unmasked him. We restored his dignity by referring to him as "Doc."

Phillip "Phiggy" Lake, 25, a member of Col. Jonathan Stevenson's New York Volunteers during the Mexican-American War.[140] Phiggy was apprenticed as a watchmaker but found the work too confining and when the opportunity to sail off to California presented itself, he took it.

The parole stipulations were such that if Doc and Phiggy even so much as *thought* of disobeying one of my orders, they immediately would be classified as "mutineers" and subject to arrest. They had the choice, of course, of rejecting or accepting the parole stipulations. But, as both men were fully apprised of the wonders of the Chinese lacquer palace through detailed conversations they had with their jailers, I felt very much as Father Christmas bearing gifts to two gleeful children.

The young ladies, I emphasized to my new recruits, were independent entrepreneurs. What they did with their time and bodies was their business, so long as it did not encumber our mission.

After their introduction to the Vista Del Mar/Monte regulars, I gave Doc and Phiggy their first assignment: to attend the Rev. Cowan's open air revival meeting.

John Cowan was one of those rare individuals who could tell an audience what God would say—word for word—had He not been called away to some distant corner of the world to administer a pestilence on a people even worse than the Monterey crowd thus assembled.

What God would have said is, "Thank you, Monterey, for your prayers. The heathen house of prostitution is about to depart for the Mexican hell hole, Sonoran Camp. There it will find a home among the wretched and depraved Papists."

Then God would have added this footnote: "The seeker after gold who places family and community and duty and honest toil behind his lust for the transient treasures of this earth, is more hated by my son, Jesus, then were the money changers in the temple."

Which was followed by a plea for a few coins to allow Rev. Cowan to continue with his struggle against evil.

---

[140] The volunteers arrived in San Francisco on March 7, 1847, and were mustered out of service the next year. Stevenson went to the mining camp of Mokelumne Hill where he was elected *alcalde*. C.H. does not give the particulars as to why these two men were in the brig. In Doc's case we might assume it had something to do with his "medical" background.

Apparently Doc was moved to exclaim, "Amen! And beings you ain't after the treasures of this earth no more, I ain't about to piss an offering in your piss-pot."

Doc, it seemed, was going to add a bit of spice to our curious enterprise. In his report he faulted Rev. Cowan first and foremost for "being a fool, for only a fool would mount a California pulpit and do a rant against gold. Holy Christ, man, what is California without its gold?"

Phiggy threw in the bait: "Perhaps we were in the presence of a true man of God, not caring for the graceless, fragile glories of this world."

"Bah!" exclaimed Doc. "I have a knowledge of the mysteries of man, and I swear that preacher is the sort Jesus hated worse than he did them damned money changers in them damned temples."

Before turning in that last night in Monterey, the Vista Del Mar/Monte safely stashed in the wagons, the ladies having folded their tents for a very rare night off, Doc and Phiggy having made their reports, the Professor standing guard on the Carmel Road, shooing away would-be patrons of Eve's Art, the subject turned to Dandelion and the rare headache she was suffering.

Doc said, "Let me see what I can do." He circled her skull with his fingers and thumbs and felt around for the bumps his training in physiognomy would give a clue as to the root of her ailment. He gave a preliminary diagnosis:

"You show signs of possessing 'large combativeness'."

"Hell's fire," said Opal, "we all knew that!"

"Do you locate combativeness in the front of the head?" I asked in complete innocence.

"Who in thunder said it was in the front of the skull?" Doc demanded.

"You rested your fingers on the front part of Dandelion's head," I said.

"Yes, possibly so," Doc answered, "but if I did my thumb

was at the same time resting on the bump of combativeness. My gracious, anyone knows that."

A further word about Milford "Doc" Brewer: He was so typical of many who deserted the East to fill the bar-rooms, billiard parlors, fandango halls and, eventually the poor farms of California. Doc had easy morals. He was friendly and even gregarious. But, he was not thrifty. He was not close to the truth in all matters. He was not necessarily clean of person. He was not constant. He did not volunteer to do an extra job. He was not industrious. He was not bothered by conscience.

He was not one who spent time thinking of ways to torture himself. He was who he was. He tipped the scale, weighted down with all his inadequacies listed above, in favor of the positive by the rarest of rare gifts which he possessed in abundance: the ability to laugh at himself. God gave him the talent for laughter. He filled our curious enterprise with spells of uproarious hilarity.

13

Companions

A word regarding prostitutes is here in order, in lieu of their conspicuous absence from the entire spectrum of Monterey society at the Fremonts' reception.

The rise of the Ancient Greek city-state provided a new interest for men whose mothers, wives, and daughters were now no longer their mental equals.

It is significant that the polite term for the Greek prostitute was "companion" (*hetaira*). Like her sister in modern Japan, the geisha, she combined mental accomplishments with attractiveness. The "companion" had to be able to enter into her male client's intellectual interests.

The Vista Del Mar/Monte ladies, companions *par excellent*, were worthy heirs to an honorable profession.

14

We Start for the Great Central Valley

We left in our six wagons in the pre-dawn, bidding farewell to the balsam wonder of the stunted pines on the Carmel Mission road.

Rick and Billy on the hay wagons; Doc, Phiggy, and the Professor on the buckboards; me driving the wagonette with the chattering ladies talking back to the birds....

Much giggling and reminiscing. One such recollecting worthy of repeating here:

A Spanish lugger laden with olive oil ran up on the beach in Monterey. To re-float the boat it would be necessary to drain off the oil, the problem being the oil was rancid. Fortunately there was at the time in these parts a "doctor" who concocted all manner of remedies for ailments ranging from rheumatism to ingrown toe nails. Rancid olive oil was something he could use and he had an empty cistern big enough to hold much of the "liquid gold."

At this very time, it so happened, Scarlet, Princess, and the irrepressible Opal were on a fortnight's sabbatical. And it also so happened the ladies wanted to rent a cottage on the olive oil doctor's beach estate. And it also also so happened that the landlord didn't want to deal with cash, but with the coin the three ladies dealt with. And, finally, also also also he wanted the payment made by all three ladies together all at once.

A "threesome" was nothing foreign to the ladies and the

idea of a "foursome" was within the bounds of possibility. That was not the hitch.

The hitch was the professor had taken a rancid olive oil immersion to test the potency of his new wonder medicine. The natural body odor of an unwashed man is bad enough, but add to it a bath in rancid olive oil, the combination was practically lethal. Recovering from the initial shock the ladies gave it another try but to no avail.

"I've had lots of men go limp on me," said Opal, "but this was the first time I went limp."

15

Pairings

We camped that first night at the Rancho Bolsa Nueva y Moro Cojo, a combination of three grants—30,901 acres of seashore land crisscrossed by a network of sloughs and swamps, not much good for anything but raising fleas and mosquitos.[141]

I was surprised to see how quickly pairings took place, answering the most fundamental human instinct, to share experience. Rick and Scarlet at the far end of the campfire were "old" chums, old in this case being B.C.—"Before Caesar"; but Billy and Daphne...that was a puzzle. Doc and Phiggy were old cell mates. They were recalling funny happenings in the Presidio brig. Princess, Gertie, and Mary Turtle-Eyes had worked together to prepare supper and continued working together, chatting about childhood foods they were fond of whose exact flavors can not be duplicated, while they cleaned up. That left Dandelion, Opal, and me to talk about a subject we had in common: Hyrum Milton, Mary Lawrence Milton, Zinfandella Milton, and—with apprehension on my part lest something be disclosed by the two women that would taint the reputation of Burgundia Milton.

Billy Tremaine and Daphne. The success of my mission

---

[141] Given in 1844 by Governor Manuel Micheltorena principally to Maria Antonia Pico de Castro, Juan Bautista Castro's mother. This is the future site of Castroville, renowned as the "Artichoke Capital of America," thanks to the Italians who settled here. An interesting fact: the annual per capita consumption of artichokes in Italy is 365—one a day! The sloughs are popular for wildfowl hunting and fishing.

depended some on preparation, some on favorable road conditions, some on the avoidance of trouble in the form of highwaymen, some on luck, and a great deal on harmony within the ranks of our company. Billy Tremaine and tall, romantic Daphne. They knew our cardinal rule, our prime "thou shalt not" — Thou shalt not have sexual intercourse within our circle.

But, late that first night on the trail, I thought I saw Billy roll out of his blankets presumably to relieve himself in the area set aside for that purpose near the tethered animals, followed, in time, by one of the ladies — Daphne. I noticed also that she carried a blanket.

We broke camp at dawn after drinking the Professor's coffee and eating a crust of Monterey bread. The sandy road led northeast away from the Pacific. I had said nothing to Billy and Daphne. With scores of miles ahead of us, I was determined to let harmony prevail. I decided to hold my fire by way of reasoning thusly: Even though we are mobile, we are still a whorehouse. Just as the tiger cannot wish away its spots neither can I wish away the fact that the young ladies making the journey in my care are whores and not novices on a final outing in the outside world prior to taking their holy vows and a cloistered life. Whores screw for a living. Screwing is what they do. But, whores also are women whose primal instinct is to nurture the young. Billy is young. Daphne was "nurturing" him. Nurturing is not against our rules.

In the early afternoon we came to a well-marked crossroads. I remembered it from my trip down to Monterey with Bayard. West would take us back to the ocean and Mission Santa Cruz. North would take us to Mission San Juan Bautista. Our itinerary was north.

A pair of horsemen — *Californios* — sat on the ground in the shade of their dozing horses. The two men got to their feet and dusted their clothing as we approached. The Professor, in the lead buckboard, reined in his mules, stepped down to the road and walked up to the duo. The Professor was not armed, the two *vaqueros* were. A brief exchange of words, the handing over to the Professor of an envelope, handshakes, and the two horsemen mounted and rode a few yards down the Mission Santa Cruz road, and waited.

"This is for you," the Professor said, handing me the envelope. The entire crew—all 12 of them—left their posts and followed the message the Professor delivered.

It was a note from Hyrum Milton: "Small change of plans. These men—Jose and Rubin—will show you where to camp. They can be trusted."

Here I must pause in my narrative to tell you why Jose and Rubin could be "trusted." Like me and no doubt scores of others in Judge Milton's jurisdiction, they were "paroled" to do a bit of work the judge needed done—Jose and Rubin, horse-thieves I later learned, to deliver a message—me to transport a whore house, whores and all, to Sonora.

We plodded along the shore-hugging road, our two Mexican guides frequently looking back over their shoulders to see that our caravan was properly moving along, but more so to survey the young women. These sightings always brought forth some comment in rapid-fire Spanish followed by appreciative laughter. The sight of Daphne in full travel regalia elicited cheers from our discriminating guides riding point.

By late afternoon we were in sight of the Mission and its ruined front wall.[142] There were few people about—no priests that I could see and only a handful of elderly Indians who had escaped the deadly diseases brought to them by the Europeans along with the gift of the holy sacrament.

---

[142] C.H. is way off the mark here. The front wall of the adobe church compound was destroyed in 1857 by the Fort Tejon Earthquake which ruptured the southern part of the San Andreas Fault for a distance of 225 miles. Mission Santa Cruz was founded in 1791 by the Franciscans and was early depleted.

The Memoirs of Caesar Honore

We were setting up for the night when Jose and Rubin reappeared. Another message from Hyrum who now, it was certain, was very close by. (He enjoyed intrigue, especially dramatic huggermuggery.)

My instructions were to follow Jose and Rubin on the saddled mount they had brought for me; that I was to come armed because Jose or Rubin, or both for that matter, might be cut-throats.

The two *desperadoes* seemed more interested in scanning the young ladies than they were in cutting my throat, so with a bit of reluctance on their part led me to the site of the rendezvous. No sooner had the sound of Jose and Rubin's hoof-prints vanished, the sound of an approaching horse was heard. The rider was a boy in britches, a tattered shirt, and a cap pulled down over his ears. He was frisking his horse, and 20 feet from my mount reigned in, causing his horse to rise up on his hind legs and proclaim majesty over the earth in general and me in particular.

This reckless maneuver caused my blood to boil. When I was able to speak, I cursed the irresponsible lad as a "Damned Fool!"...one who should have a "razor strop redden your miserable arse."

16

Burgundia (1)

The young rider spoke: "How I misjudged you, Caesar. Your letters were full of loving concern, and now I learn you want to take a strop to my behind!"

Burgundia! It was Burgundia. The cap came off and her golden hair cascaded down to rest on her shoulders.

"Leave it to Hyrum Milton to think of everything," I said as I rode to be at her side.

"You wouldn't want me to be lariated by a highwayman," she said innocently, but as she spoke I heard her armed escorts stationed in the underbrush depart the scene.

We were alone.

The dance began.

"Pity the highwayman," I said.

Burgundia laughed at that. "And what of the casual stranger in San Francisco?" she asked.

"You need not fear him," I said.

"Why? Am I so unattractive?"

"You are most attractive."

"What then? Could it be this San Francisco stranger fears my father?"

"He is formidable and his tentacles reach to the furthest corners of California."

"Would I be here alone with a San Francisco stranger if he had disapproved?"

"No—I mean yes—I respect...I mean...."

"You mean you can't figure out why he allowed this...."

"That's what I mean."

"I'm not always going to be around to tell you what it is you mean."

Burgundia was tying my thoughts into knots. Of course, she could have done as much by simply being with me and not saying a word.

Burgundia!

Our horses were walking down the road side-by-side. Great Heavens! Was the entire world in love?

I reached out and took Burgundia's hand. She did not withdraw it.

She continued the conversation, but went down a different track: "Are the young ladies attractive? I've never met them."

"Would your father allow it?"

"Are they attractive?"

"My fondest wish would be that you ask that question because you are jealous...."

She hooted so loudly the horses gave a start: "Jealous! It is they who should be jealous of me!!!"

I was misunderstood. I meant that I would be flattered if Burgundia was jealous of the ladies being with me....

No use. She would not be pacified until our horses had taken three dozen steps.

I began again: "Burgundia...."

"My father," she interrupted, "prides himself in being a great judge of character. Of course, when he is wrong in estimating a person, he forgets that particular incident. When he is right he shouts his success to the heavens."

"How has he judged me?" I asked, steering our conversation back to the main point of our arranged encounter—prepared by the master puppeteer.

"Frankly, I am getting a bit weary of hearing you praised at our breakfast table, lunch table, and evening meal table," said Burgundia. "Last week my mother asked 'Is this young man a man or a god?'"

"I spent less than a month with your family preparing for this curious enterprise...."

"He has spies," Burgundia said. "Are you not aware of the reports he receives from Monterey and every other place he has an interest in? I've read some of the Monterey letters. They are written by a woman who could give us a lesson in parsing."

"It must be wonderful having parents who have complete confidence in their daughter," I said.

"Are you being sarcastic?" Burgundia asked.

"No," I answered. "I admire the assurance...."

"What of your parents?" she interrupted.

"I, too, am blessed," I said. "I only hope I can be as good a parent to my children as they are to me."

"The family!" Burgundia cried out by way of a salute.

"*La famiglia!*" I answered.

At that moment we each became aware of our fates: together to create a new family. Hyrum Milton had decided on it. He allowed his daughter a final out — this rendezvous — on the matter. But, marriage — the creation of a union that would last to the very end of time — was too important to be left in the hands of children.

Hyrum Milton had set up the sternest hurdle for a candidate for his daughter's virginity to surmount: to travel with seven beautiful courtesans — and not so much as make a carnal remark, let alone initiate an overt act toward them. Hyrum knew the details of the Mabel Clark affair. Indeed, had there not been a Mabel Clark, Hyrum would have questioned my masculinity.

It was getting late and I had a tricky ride finding my way back to the Vista Del Monte camp. Burgundia relayed these instructions: "Daddy says if after being with you this evening, I concur with his judgment regarding your character, I am to invite you to spend the night in the adobe we had taken so that you and he can meet in the morning to discuss Vista Del Monte business."

"And what if you find me lacking?" I asked.

"In that event I am to bid you good-night, and in the morning Daddy will ride over to your camp, give you payment for services rendered to date, and terminate your employment."

17

Burgundia (2)

I awakened to the soft shuffling sounds of a house preparing for a new day. Fires were being stoked, orders given and acknowledged.

From down the long hallway leading to the back room where I had been given a bed came the gentle sound of feet shuffling. Burgundia, in night clothes, slipped into the room. The pupils of her eyes were large as they sought to adjust themselves to the darkness.

All had been decided. She slid into the bed beside me. Her night gown rolled up over her hips and when I sought to embrace her the back of my hand slid across the wetness of her sex, causing her to utter a primeval song of passion.

The first probe at ending her virginity caused her to cry out sharply, and we returned to the coldness of reality.[143]

"We must stop here," I said. "Yes," she answered.

---

[143] Confucius says a child should never think upon the sexual activity of his parents, and I suppose that extends also to grandparents. C.H. and Burgundia were such vital people, I think it only adds to their humanism to know the details of their first passion. This was certainly a case of deep love from the beginning. This was not an age of public display of affection. I have heard tell from several sources that they were the most handsome couple in all of California. "People would gasp when they entered a room," R. G, Collins, the *Chronicle* religion editor, told me. "They looked like the rest of us wished we looked.

18

Milford "Doc" Brewer, Ole Bull, and Our "Decameron"

The fact that her daughter may or may not have lost her virginity under her roof seems not to have fazed Mary Lawrence Milton. I was made welcome, and we exchanged pleasantries. She was a remarkable woman whose hallmark was frankness — a quality handed down to Burgundia. If Mary Lawrence had one flaw it was her flightiness — a charming trait in her youth, but rather irksome in later life.[144]

That particular long-ago morning Hyrum was at the Mission. She thinks he had an interest in buying it. I was to be fed and then escorted by Jose and Rubin back to the Vista Del Monte camp where Hyrum would meet us with some sort of intelligence regarding our itinerary.

Under no circumstance was Burgundia to leave the house.

Repeat: Burgundia was to stay with her mother and the servants.

---

[144] Here C.H. does not exaggerate. Great-Grandmother Milton was notorious for her forgetfulness, and on one supreme occasion at the Palace, did the following: 1) Arrived an hour late for a Red and Blue luncheon that she was hosting; 2) Dressed in orange and yellow although rule one in the organization's bylaws was that all members wear red and blue to official functions; 3) Forgot her dentures; 4) Mistook the porter for the husband of the Red and Blue's organist, and talked to him for a quarter- hour on the subject of out-of-tune pianos; 5) Left the Palace on the arm of the Civil War hero James Duncan as he ambled out into the street to lead a fund-raising rally for the wounded and maimed.

There was, I was soon to learn in the most pleasing manner, a second guest at the Milton adobe that morning. He made his presence known by the strains of violin music floating through the house.

"It's Ole Bull," whispered Mary Lawrence Milton. "He wanted to see more of California than the cityscape, so we brought him along."

Ole Bull emerged into the kitchen—a wild-haired, raw-boned gentleman wearing a long black frock coat despite the time of day and the setting not being a concert hall. He carried a yellow violin. Mary Lawrence attempted the introductions, but Burgundia stepped in to help: "Mr. Bull, I'd like you to meet my fiancé Caesar Honore. Caesar, this is Ole Borneman Bull, the famous Norwegian violinist and composer."

If I may be permitted, at this time, to relate a second meeting we had with Ole Bull, which may prove of interest to music lovers. (I will return to the "fiancé" portion of Burgundia's introduction later.)

It seems Ole Bull was giving a concert in San Francisco. The concert hall was packed, including the Milton-Honore clan. The stern violinist silenced his audience with a scold, and began playing. The music was exquisite. While every breath in that hall was suspended, and every ear attentive to catch the sounds of his magical instrument, the silence was broken and the harmony harshly interrupted by a voice all too familiar to me.

Milford "Doc" Brewer, having studied far too many phrenologist lumps of "large combativeness," stood up and shouted, "None of your high-falutin, but give us 'Hail Columbia' and bear hard on the treble!"

Shouts of "Turn him out!" were heard from every corner of the house. Hall employees rushed forward to remove my outspoken friend. Doc was an athlete incognito and it was a difficult task for the forces of law, order, and decency to overpower him, although they used fists and billy-clubs in their effort to do him up.

I told Burgundia to stick with her family. I was going to be on hand to make bail for Doc.

"Tell him for me," said Burgundia, "I, too, wasn't much taken with Ole Bull's selection. 'Hail Columbia' would have been nice."[145]

Back to Burgundia's engagement announcement. In recounting this story over the years, she always ends the narrative with: "You should have seen Caesar's face!!!"

Hyrum Milton's news was dire. There was much *bandito* activity in the Mission San Juan Bautista area. That location was key to getting to the Pacheco Pass[146] and the Central Valley beyond.

He was sending his family and Ole Bull back to San Francisco that very morning. I was to move the Vista Del Monte caravan to the adobe, where we were to lay low until ordered to resume our odyssey. Meanwhile, he and Rick would go into Santa Cruz to hire a few more *pistoleros*.

If the ladies so desired they could work out of their canvas tents. It was up to them. Dandelion would run that operation.

But first, as was Hyrum's custom, we had a "Big Palaver." The barbarians could be knocking at the gate and Hyrum would insist that we sit around in a circle and discuss our options and assess our chances. Because Rev. Cowan's future son-in-law was in our cortege—and Hyrum knew it—he gave explicit orders to not use his name in our deliberations; he was to be introduced to the newcomers as "George VanSaake."

"I want to know about Zachary Fenner," Hyrum said.

---

[145] Ole Bull was indeed the greatest concert violinist of his age, but it is a certainty he never performed in California. The incident that C.H. recounts re "Hail Columbia" is a true story—but it happened in Washington D. C., and the music critic was a Congressman. Ole Bull acquired a large tract of land in Pennsylvania in 1852 and founded a colony there.

146 The Pass was an important east-west link between the Coast and the Great Central Valley. The Butterfield Overland Mail ran this route from 1858 to 1881.

Surely, I thought, he knew all there was to know about his hired enemy. "I took him to be a good sort. When the time comes I'll straighten him out," he added.

"That's your trouble," said Dandelion. "Everyone is a 'good sort' to you."

Hyrum: "Why revenge an enemy when you can outwit him?[147]

Abrupt change of subject: "I understand some of you are coupling-up," Hyrum said. "That's wonderful, but that's also a potential heap of trouble. Wait until the Vista Del Monte is up and running."

Next subject: the Brownell Sawmill a mile from the adobe. Hyrum bought it in March, 1849; sold it 30 days later to a Jasper Brown who converted the name to Brown Sawmill by dropping the "ell." Hyrum wanted to know if anyone present would be interested in buying it for it again belonged to him by way of two foreclosures.

"No takers? Fine. We will go on to the next order of business: Monterey."

Monterey? "What about Monterey?" Mary Turtle-Eyes asked.

Hyrum explained: "California — the State of California — will be run by the likes of the men who are in Monterey for the Constitutional Convention. These men will make laws — mostly against certain practices.[148] Prostitution comes to mind. Did any of your customers give you their names? That would be valuable information to have when it came time to vote to close down the bordellos."

The ladies looked at one another, sharing uneasy demeanors.

---

[147] A quote from Xolotl.

[148] Indeed. The very first law passed by the California State Legislature banned Indians from setting fire to underbrush, which was their centuries' old agricultural practice. By burning the rank underbrush they would insure that come the following spring the vegetation would be lush. White miners were dying of scurvy, a disease caused by the lack of Vitamin C.

Scarlet spoke: "That's something we don't do, nor would do. That would be contrary to our rules."

"Rules?" asked Phiggy.

"The world's oldest profession would never have survived the centuries if we didn't have rules," said Dandelion.

Hyrum was going after bigger game—protecting the world's oldest profession from potential hypocrites who might seek to strangle it with a noose made of their newly minted laws.

"Was Zachary Fenner one of your clients or any of the other delegates?" Hyrum asked.

Silence.

We were no sooner settled in at the adobe when Rick returned with three of the meanest looking *hombres* this side of the Rio Grande. One was missing an ear—*prima facie* evidence that he had been caught stealing and so branded with the earectomy. The ladies instinctively moved into the shadows.

That evening sitting around the campfire Rick told us of his recruiting adventure:

"George knew about these fellows from the sawmill and he knew they spent most of their leisure time—which was all the time when the mill was broke and waiting for parts—at a *cantina* run by one of George's 'good friends'—Hell, everybody up and down the coast is his good friend—

"George sees these three birds at the back of the bar-room and yells, 'Fire in the head,' which means George is going to buy everyone in this dump a drink.

"The bartender—this son-of-a-bitch is missing both ears!—perks up and begins pouring. George greets him by name and introduces me to 'Short-bit Manuel'."[149]

And so began in that far away time an evening of entertainments to rival Boccaccio's *Decameron*.[150] Briefly noted are the tales I recall after Rick's account in the *cantina*:

Doc: "When I was practicing medicine one of my regulars comes in and I tell him he is looking great. 'Keep this up,' I tell him, 'and I wouldn't be surprised to see you live to be 70.' 'But, I am 70,' this chap says. 'See,' I say, 'what did I tell you?'"

Phiggy: "I'm up in Canada working in a fine hotel. My boss giving me the job's particulars. Most important thing he says is having tact. I don't know tact from a sour lemon. He explains. He has to deliver a message to room 17. The door is ajar so he walks in and there stands a naked woman. 'Pardon me, sir,' I say, making a quick turnaround. A week passes. I see the boss and tell him I was able to use tact. I had to deliver some drinks to room 5. I walk in and there's this guy atop this woman, screwing away. I walk over and tap him on his arse and ask, 'Which one of you gentlemen ordered the Amaranto vermouth?'"

Opal: "Little girl tells her Mommy that she's getting fat. 'But remember,' says the Mommy, 'Mommy has a baby growing in her tummy.' 'Yeah,' says the little girl, 'but what's that growing in your arse?'"

Scarlet: "Grizzlies used to be a big problem here. This miner was giving the tenderfoot some advice, like wearing tiny bells on his pack to give the bears time to clear out. But, says the old timer, grizzlies can't be relied on to clear out: 'If you see grizzly droppings on the trail, clear out.' The tenderfoot wants to know how you can tell if they're grizzly bear droppings. 'That's easy,' says the old-timer, 'they're full of small bells.'"

Dandelion: "This midget goes into one of them bordellos on the Barbary Coast. When he's leaving he is surprised to be handed a $20 gold piece. He goes back the next night and same thing—another $20. Same thing the night after that. But

---

[149] At that time whiskey sold for two shots for a quarter—or one shot for fifteen cents. A man who lays down his short-bit on the bar for a solitary shot is the object of scorn and quickly earns the derisive name of "Short Dime Joe" or "Short Bit Harry."

[150] The 14th Century Florentine writer Giovanni Boccaccio's collection of novellas is set in a secluded villa where seven young women and three young men have gone to escape the Black Plague.

on the fourth night — nothing. 'How come?' he wants to know. 'We only run the peep show on Mondays, Tuesdays, and Wednesdays,' explains the doorman."

Mary Turtle-Eyes: "This beautiful woman is sitting in a *cantina* when a drunk comes up to her and says, 'I've got a couple of dollars and it looks like you could use the money.' The woman answers: 'What makes you think I charge by the inch?'"

Me: "This beautiful woman walks into the room and sits down next to this fellow. 'I see you are interested,' she says. 'For twenty dollars I'll do anything you want.' 'Anything?' asks the fellow, so struck by the woman's beauty he can hardly get the words out. 'Anything,' she repeats but with one condition: 'You'll have to tell me in only three words what you want me to do.' The man thinks a while, slides a $20 gold piece to her, and says, 'Paint my house.'"

Billy: "This happened to me aboard the *Tronka*. I don't think Caesar ever heard it told. The ship was a clipper which means she was long and narrow and built for speed. That speed was measured in so many knots per hour and the owners take great boastful pride in how fast their ship is. Speed is measured by using a chip log wooden panel attached by line to a reel. Knots are placed on the line at a distance of eight fathoms. If the ship is cruising along at 'top' speed there is no need to wrestle with the canvas. The crew can rest easy. If we're going slower than top then it's all hands on deck, climb the rigging and put on more canvas. So we got together and did an alteration job on the line. The knots were re-tied to intervals of less than eight knots."

Princess: "These two men walk into a one-woman whorehouse. The first one comes out and says, 'Heck, my wife is better than that.' The second one has a go and when he comes out he says to his dear friend, 'You're right. Your wife is better.'"

Daphne: "I've never told this story before. It's true and it happened to me. My randy cousin got me started when I was only twelve. You know that story. He had money and he was always buying me nice clothes. I tried my best to pay him back by pretending I liked what he was doing to me. Some of it was good, but mostly it hurt. He was a big man, I'd guess three hundred pounds. When he finished he couldn't move off me and sometimes I was certain I would suffocate. Well, the last time he did me he was the one who suffocated. He died right on top of me and I couldn't move him off. I knew he was dead, and I knew if I didn't get some help I would die too. My cousin's wife is the one who found us. 'I knew you were the one screwing LeRoy,' she shouted at me. 'Little whore screwing my man for pretty clothes.' It was terrible. My folks, my brothers and sisters, all in the room screaming at me. My sister Imogene throwing my clothes in a satchel, my father cursing me. I was twelve years old."

The Professor: "This *hombre* and his son go away to Texas and after ten years they go home to Mexico. Just outside the town the father is tired and he tells the boy to go into town and have some fun. The next day the father asks the boy did he have fun? '*Si*,' says the boy. "I screwed this lady who lives in a yellow and white house and raises monkeys and has a black mole on her chin, one on her forehead, and two on her tits." '*Carumba*,' says the father. "You screwed my mother!' 'So what?' says the boy, 'You are always screwing my mother.'"

Gertie: "I went home one time since I've been doing this. I told my parents I was a convent teacher in a cloistered Catholic order and this was my last bit of freedom before I took the veil. My parents are strict Baptists. They were shocked at me being a Catholic nun. I'll never forget what my father said: 'I'd sooner you told us you were a prostitute than to learn that you have become a Papist.' Now there's a real-son-of-a-bitch."

That being the last page of the Vista Del Monte version of the *Decameron*, we crawled under our blankets, praying for Gertie and Daphne.

19

Over the Pacheco Pass

Having received word that the *banditos* had moved on, the Vista Del Monte caravan reached Mission San Juan Bautista,[151] a much livelier settlement at the foot of the Pacheco Pass and California's Great Central Valley. Our lacquered boards and painted ladies drew much attention, openly relished by Opal, Billy, and Doc, but of serious concern to me. The *alcalde* shared my apprehension, and so did an imposing 40-year-old *Californio* with sideburns and a grand *mustachio*: General Jose Castro.[152] It was "suggested" that we keep moving, there being no troops garrisoned here, the nearest 40 miles north in the Pueblo of San José, or the same distance south in Monterey.

I suggested to Rick that we deputize two or three additional outriders. When he made the announcement three-quarters of the male citizens of San Juan Bautista jostled forward for a job interview. I could not tell whether this ardor to serve came from

---

[151] Here, at last, C.H. uses the ablative case to move his narrative along. The ablative is used in various languages to express motion away from something. For instance: Caesar reaches the Rubicon. The next sentence reads, "Having crossed the Rubicon...." The reader is spared all the steps in between, such as the soldiers choosing trees to fell, building pontoon bridges, etc.

[152] Castro was born in Monterey in 1808 making him one of those rare native-born birds to govern Alta California (1835-36). He then became *Commandante General* of the Mexican Army at the time of the Bear Flag Revolt and the Mexican-American War. No friend of the Americans, Castro advocated California be annexed by Great Britain. Aside from the mission, the most imposing structure in San Juan Bautista is the two-story Castro House. The bandit Marguez assassinated Castro in 1860.

a desire to return to the diggings in relative comfort and style, or whether the chance to be in the company of females was the prime motivating factor.[153]

There is, alas, no way to prevent the occasional flare-up that occurs when you place in close day-by-day proximity nearly two-dozen people, from nearly two-dozen different planets, with nearly two-dozen different personal dreams.

The incident that sticks out in my mind took place on the Pacheco Pass at a mud-and-canvas liquor mill bearing the unlikely name, "The Civilian," and concerning Doc, the most likely of our group to get in a scrape.

We were forced by the fatigue of our animals to make camp across the road from The Civilian. I gave strict orders—the ladies were confined to camp, and if any of our men wanted to taste the high life of Pacheco Pass they were to go in the company of a partner. No solo venturers into this den of inequity.

Doc and Phiggy (I should have added a codicil to my decree that these two could not form a team) were the first to hitch up their trousers and enter The Civilian. I deemed it my duty to tag along as chaperone.

The Mexican patrons, a half-dozen of them, fell silent when we three *gringos* made our appearance. Doc sought out the proprietor and asked in a loud voice: "How in hell did you come to name this fleatrap The Civilian? That's a Yankee name and all I see here are a bunch of Greasers."

Even Phiggy gasped. I diffused the situation by stating in simple Spanish, hand gestures, and broken English that my

---

[153] Stories abound on the effects of the imbalance of the sexes in the early days of the Gold Rush, and to the great lengths male miners went to be in the company of a female. Most of the early Argonauts, having no intention of settling in California after making their fortunes, left their wives at home. In time, as California's appeal as a place to live grew, more and more wives came West. At the very start of the Gold Rush, women like the Vista Del Mar's septuplets, euphemistically classified as "entertainers," were the majority of European descendant non-Hispanic women.

friend had just received his wages and wanted to treat the house and especially the Mexican *amigos* at the far table to a drink of the house's best. This was universally understood, and in simple Spanish, hand gestures, and broken English the proprietor revealed the secret of The Civilian. The prior owner was in San Francisco one day on the flats where scores of derelict ships were slowly sinking in the mud. One of them sported a handsomely lettered nameplate—just the right size for the saloon he had in mind to build, so he ripped it off the ship's stern and walked away with the vessel's identity.

Doc was uncharacteristically quiet. "What's this 'been paid my wages' business?" he asked.

"Just what it means," I said. "The drinks cost me exactly what you were owed to date."

He said nothing, but when we walked through the door he let loose the loudest fart ever rendered in these parts by man or beast. That punctuating exit became famous in the diggings, and I can say, with a modicum of pride, that I was there.

The 12-mile-long pass follows a canyon, the trail leading over hills of quite sufficient altitude. On every side we could look off into bottomless distances. Our mules, especially those having to move the hay wagons, were nearly spent, and as there was no replacements in this wild pass, gave me great concern.

The situation eased a bit when we passed the crest[154] and started the descent into the broad San Joaquin Valley, affording me my first look at the distant snow-capped Sierra Nevada Mountains.[155] At the eastern end of the Pass is the San Luis Ranch, the only habitation within 30 north or south miles, and a great rendezvous site for drovers. Their cattle dotted the plain.

The ranch featured a large dining room, but it was not

---

[154] The elevation is 1368 feet.
[155] It must have been an exceptional day. There are precious few of them when the Great Central Valley haze or fog does not hide the eastern mountains from view.

large enough to accommodate our numbers, so we dined in shifts. Doc was in the first shift, still holding sway for his fellow Vista Del Monte cohorts and the few other guests at supper when we of the second shift walked in. Doc's melodious tones settled on the subject of Indians: "...the Indian poses the immediate threat...."

"Bah," exclaimed one of the diners, "The Indian has been reduced to the status of a starving beggar. What say you to that?"

"What I say, Sir," said Doc, "is that stupidity has no friends, and wants none."

20

The California Constitutional Convention Ends

On October 13—the day we departed Monterey—the California Constitutional Convention came to a happy end. The last of the delegates signed the document, and General Riley ordered a 31-gun salute, in anticipation of California becoming the thirty-first state in the Union.

Bayard, who gave me these accounts when we met for the final time in San Francisco, told me that John Sutter declared: "Gentlemen, this is the happiest day of my life...a great day for California." How bitter would be those words in the wrinkled throat of that old fool[156] as he spends his old age in Washington City seeking recompense for the kingdom on the Sacramento River which was taken from him by the ant-like Yankee invading miners and merchants and agriculturists.

Like true politicians, the delegates had ordered $16-per-day pay for themselves, plus $16 per mile travel expense. This was paid to them in silver coin from the Monterey customs house treasury.

J. Ross Brown, clerk of the Convention, was given $10,000 to print up the Convention's Report both in English and Spanish, as mandated by the treaty with Mexico.

The voters—12,000 to 800—approved the Constitution; Sutter's former assistant Peter H. Burnett was elected Governor as predicted, and the Legislature named Fremont and William

[156] C.H. is uncharacteristically unkind with this remark. He did not care for Sutter's lifestyle, especially when he designed and wore a military-style uniform.

M. Gwin the state's Senators.

Before Fremont went to the Capital to push for California's admission into the Union, his 70-square-mile "worthless" ranch in Mariposa turned out to be a golden cornucopia.[157]

We Vista Del Mar folk missed the grand ball held in Monterey to celebrate completion of the Constitution — as if it is likely we would have been invited. Opal's observation gave us a bit of balm: "They did not want us there because they were afraid we'd stand in the reception line and greet the high and mighty muck-a-mucks with 'Hello, Charlie, I've screwed you' and 'There's George, I've screwed him' and 'Ole Silent Sam — he had me doggy-style four or five times' and 'John — isn't he the one that tried to stick a beer bottle up Gertie's arse?'"

Meanwhile, I had a foot in another world: Burgundia. Her letters caught up to me, but, frankly at that stage in our relationship, provided me with little comfort. She wrote of a new dance academy some spinster from Massachusetts — "Did I know her? She thinks she knows you." — organized for the sprinkling of young people in need of the East's social advantages. There were some handsome young military officers who attended the dances, but never enough to go around. The rest of the males were young and mostly foolish.

She described her new gown in detail.

Her letters made no concealed hint of our brief but momentous contact. It was real — and beautiful. Did it mean nothing to her?

Burgundia was on the verge of becoming the social queen of Alta California — the right appearance, the right connections, the right time, the right place, the right bloodline, the right clothes, the right intellect, the right social grace.... And she was working on her only deficiency — ballroom dancing!

And I....

---

[157] Not quite. Fremont was never able to gain clear title to the Spanish land grant.

21

Joaquin

"The Duchess of Kent is paying a visit to some wounded British soldiers recently back from the wars. 'What ails you, my good man?' she asks one of the injured patients. 'It's me private parts, Mum,' he answers. 'Oh,' she sez, 'A broken bone?' The soldier sez, 'Me compliments to the Duke.'"

Opal's story sends the assembled troops to their stations with a smile. Smiles were needed as we started off across the Great Valley floor. Ominous clouds were gathering; the rainy season was upon us. Our late start from Monterey and our Santa Cruz detour caused us to lose precious time.

Great swaths of tule grass[158] waved in the morning breeze, as if sending a challenge to those bent on reaching the far mountains to the east.

The Professor, in the lightest buckboard, took the point. The heavy hay wagons went to the rear. The road, such as it was, had been marked by horses. If wagons had traveled on it we could see no evidence of such pioneering work. If the Professor's buckboard was swallowed up by a mud hole, we could work it to solid ground. But, if a hay wagon became mired it would take a better part of a day to unload the Vista Del Monte's lacquered sidings before we could extract the vehicle.

And that, I'm sorry to say, is exactly what happened. The Professor's buckboard and nearly the Professor himself gradually sank in a mud hole. The lead mule drowned.

---

[158] Tule grass is a freshwater marsh plant which gets its name from the Nahuati word *tõillin* for the plants growing in Mexico City.

As we worked to extract the buckboard, the ladies set up camp. Our dinner menu was set: barbecued[159] mule.

Our fire attracted more than moths. Out of the darkness emerged a dozen Mexican *banditos* with *pistolas* drawn and cocked. Even Doc was at a loss for words.

The outriders, away from our camp at that time, fled on foot through the overgrown weeds. We never saw them again.

The leader was a small man, a whiskered Mexican wearing an embroidered skull cap.

This was Joaquin.

To the Americans, he was a cut-throat villain. To the Mexicans he was a national patriot, the "Robin Hood of El Dorado," a man justifiably seeking revenge upon the Yankees who raped his wife, lynched his half-brother, and horsewhipped him.[160]

"*Señor Murrieta*," I said. "*Bienvenidas*."

He spoke a bit of English. I understood most of it, but the pistol pointed at my head I understood completely.

"This is the *casa de las putas*," he said. "On the way to *ciudad Sonora*? You know me?"

"I know you by *reputación*," I said. "You are now a *famosos Californiano* like Sutter and Pico and Fremont and Castro and Vallejo. And besides, it is not every man who can afford to wear a shabby coat."[161]

Joaquin interrupted my spiel with a wave of his pistol. "Children speak in Italian, ladies speak in French, soldiers speak in German, God speaks in Spanish, and the devil speaks in English," he said.

"I do not speak for *el diablo*," I said. "Your Mexican

---

[159] Actually a barbecue is grilling a *whole* animal.

[160] In 1858 John Ridge wrote a dime novel on the life of Joaquin Murrieta to further muddle the facts regarding the life of this feared outlaw. The consensus is that Joaquin died in 1854 and that his head was stuck in a jar of alcohol and displayed throughout the state for a small fee.

[161] I have absolutely no idea what C.H. is saying here.

compatriots liken you to Napoleon Bonaparte."[162] This was a lie I manufactured out of thin air.

The Professor stepped forward. "*Yo soy Pablo Perez de Hermosillo. Estos personas son gente de alta estima,*" he said, apparently to good effect. The *bandito e sus hombres* lowered their guns.

As all this was taking place, the young ladies were keenly aware that they were in for a busy night. Dandelion slid a hand in a pocket and came up with a rouge stick. After a slight bit of dabbing, she passed it on to her fellow courtesans with military precision. This was a war of survival, and they were making ready their heavy artillery.

The maneuver did not escape Joaquin's attention. "These *chicas,*" he asked, "are *monjas?*"

This gave rise to a violent roar of laughter from Joaquin's troops.

Dandelion walked up to Joaquin, and with the Professor as her interpreter, said the following:

"No, we are not nuns. We are whores. We offer you our hospitality and our food. We pay our way through life by selling our bodies. It is an honorable exchange. We can tell from the way your men are acting that they are more than ready to find a soft, sweet nest for their rampant cocks. We are ready to provide that nest. All we ask is that when you are through, you leave us in peace."

It turned out to be a long, long night. Joaquin did not participate. All of his men gave their partners a gratuity.

I had never before witnessed the way the young ladies operated around male "clients." Given names were exchanged. No coyness or faked interest, curiosity, or concern. Dandelion's girls were in charge. The fondling and kissing

---

[162] Apparently C.H. did not share his generation's esteem for the French emperor. "Military genius, my aching arse," he told me. Anyone can be a genius if he can get a few thousand people to die for him." No use picking apart the logic of that statement. I said nothing.

would take place out of sight of the others. A handshake sealed the transaction.

Once alone the young women were at the mercy of their customers, except for their first line of defense—long, sharp fingernails that could rake a misbehaving man's back, affording enough time for Rick to respond. A naked man was no match to a robust man dressed head to toe in buckskin.

22

Trouble With the "Law"

Joaquin's adventure behind us, the Professor's buckboard in good repair, we continued east to the foothills.

On our last night on the flatlands we were no sooner finished with the chore of taking care of the animals (everyone, including the young ladies, participated in this nightly ritual) when we had a visit from the law and the following one-sentence order:

"Clear them whores out of this jurisdiction."

The party delivering the mandate was armed, and obviously itching for a confrontation.

I suppose of all human failings, hypocrisy rankles me the most. I have seen an abundance of it in California, perhaps because in a frontier society so many different classes of people must by force have a great deal of interaction with one another. The solid social patterns of more settled areas are not yet formed, and where it exists hypocrisy is more deftly masked.

The chief visitor was a pock-marked, mustachioed ex-sailor named William Anderson, who announced that he was the *magistrado* of this "county" and as such, was "the law."

I was to learn later that Anderson, having once held a law book in his hand, was deemed the leader in these parts of an effort to replace the Mexican system of "trial by *concilliación*" with the Anglo-Saxon "trial by jury."

Unfortunately for all who entered Anderson's bar of justice, whether he be Yankee or Mexican or Feejee Islander, the judge was usually drunk.

This was the same Anderson who, when under the influence, ordered a horse thief be executed; and later, when sober, wished to resume the trial. The Sheriff had concealed the prisoner and pretended he had carried out the harsh sentence.

"Never mind," said the sober Anderson, "proceed with the trial. All orders and judgments of this court must be justified by due and legal proceedings had."

Can one believe such men actually were permitted to fill important positions in our local governments? And now this same person was poking around the possessions of the Vista Del Monte.

The young ladies—survivors—quietly repaired to the wagonette.

"How long you girls been whoring?" Anderson asked. No answer.

He poked me with his cane. "How long you been pimping?" he asked.

I could feel the defiance rising in my being, but Dandelion, a veteran of such encounters, defused the situation by acting the whore. Her slouch and grimaces transformed her into the caricature of a vulgar hag.

"Be easy on us," she whined. "It's been a hard day. We'll be on our way before sun-up."

A woman in California in 1850, be she a saint or a sinner, was accorded some degree of respect by virtue of her scarcity, even by the likes of an Anderson.

The "law" had come to our camp seeking an agreement as to "terms," he having mistakenly supposed that we planned to settle in his "jurisdiction."

"You'll be on your way to where?" he asked.

Apparently he was the only person in the central part of California who had never heard of the Vista Del Mar's metamorphosing into the Vista del Monte.

"We're going to try our luck in Sonoran Camp," Dandelion said.

"With all them Greasers," said Anderson. These were his parting words.

The judge's departure sent us to bed in a holiday spirit. We were in sight of our goal. Daphne and Billy, Rick and Scarlett, Opal and Doc, Phiggy and Gertie—it was no use attempting to enforce the "no fraternizing" edict. Nature will out.

Among our regulars that left the Professor, Mary Turtle-Eyes, Dandelion, Princess—and me—out in the cold. All it would have taken was one word—but that word was not uttered. It remained unsaid, buried in my being by constant and recurring thoughts of Burgundia. Infidelity, like death, admits of no degrees.

Burgundia! How I had shamed and degraded her. What was the torment of her existence if mine was unbearable?

And mingled with these dark thoughts was the remembrance of the feel and sight of her virgin flesh, the passion in her breasts....

Great God! What a confusion is love!

23

In the Foothills

We were now in the foothills. At a thick cluster of oaks on a wide, green river[163] we laid over for a day to rest the animals and ourselves. Our goal was now only 50 miles away, due east. We had a chance to wash off the grime that accumulated on our trip across the valley floor, but the young ladies disdained from bathing in the river. Sunlight, I fear, they treated as an enemy. The sun's rays aged those who could not escape them.

We met our first "booster." "We got a live town here," he said. As far as I could tell he was the lone spark amidst about two dozen dead coals that made up the settlement's total population. From what I could see the "live town" on the high bank above the river consisted mainly of a corral built of heavy pine timbers, the aforementioned two dozen "houses," a half-dozen vacant miner's dog-huts, and a trading post with little inventory. A leaky plank ferry provided the sole reason for the town's existence.[164]

---

[163] The Stanislaus after the Miwok-Yokut Estanislao, a Mission San José *majordomo* who led 300 armed Indians to the river. From that stronghold they twice fought off Mexican soldiers.

[164] This no doubt was a ferry crossing at Oakdale, but records indicate that town was not settled until 1871. The road from Stockton drove southeast to French Camp and then more south than east across the Stanislaus at several places, including Riverbank, Oakdale, and Knight's Ferry. If the incident C.H. describes here had taken place at Knight's Ferry, he no doubt would have so indicated, for that settlement was well-known, and was for a time county seat of Stanislaus County when that county was formed from the western portion of Tuolumne County.

The road arrived here from Stockton, an important port city. The road then follows the river on its south bank to Sonoran Camp.

In the trading post was enthroned a shrewd Yankee surrounded by nearly naked Indians,[165] and exposing for sale jerked beef at a dollar a pound; flour at a dollar and a half; and enough trinkets and junk to have purchased the whole of the United States at Manhattan Island prices. The Indians were trading gold for raisins—straight across, ounce for ounce—a shameful practice, but not shameful enough for Billy and Doc. They made plans to trade some bits of colored glass for gold, but before they could embark on the road to making their fortunes I closed them down. From Monterey to Sonora our watchword was honesty in all our dealings. To cheat Indians at this river crossing could come back to hurt us in some unforeseen situation. We were vulnerable. We were selling sin—but at least we would sell it honestly, above board.

Conscience dictated that I put in a word favoring the Indians being deceived at the Trading Post. I asked Billy and Doc to accompany me.

My admonition was received with icy indignation. A fellow townsman, his Adam's apple twitching nervously, said, "Them's his Injuns."

"His Indians!" said Doc, showing relief for being on the right side in this argument, "Them's God's Injuns."

"God ain't got no part in this affair," said the Trader.

A second townsman, a short, fat man in black suspenders, entered the fray: "Joshua here feeds them Injuns and lets them bed down on his place."

"Appears like Joshua does more than feed and house the Indians," I said, indicating with a glance two young Indian girls sitting on the floor.

Joshua became enraged. "Who are you to moralize?" he shouted. "A whore-monger, that's who."

---

[165] No doubt Yokuts. The Miwok lived at the higher elevation.

"At least," I said, "we give honest value for honest payment. We don't weigh raisins against gold."

As we left the Trading Post we heard the Yankee's voice rise above the hubbub: "Forget it for now, boys. Let the damned fools feed the Injuns tonight. Tomorrow that train'll be gone and the Injuns'll be back at my counter...."

24

Burgundia's Letter

Caesar:

Your letter arrived via Stockton bringing the good news that you have successfully navigated the flat California valley and are within site of your goal. I dare say by the time you get this letter you will have arrived.

Things are quite the same here. The highlight being a dinner visit from your parents who are well and eager to get word that you are well as well. (My! Three "wells" in one sentence—not so well!) By "dinner visit" I mean your mother took over our kitchen, insisted that I learn the culinary art, and together with our cook produced the meal.

She related how she had once fed *ravioli–con–passero* to the great Daniel Webster and she would now show our cook and me how to prepare a different sort of "bird"—*rolladi*—"*beef birds.*"[166] Daddy said they were "marvelous" which pleased Carolina tremendously.

I have a new love in my life. It is a pianoforte[167] upon which I am learning to make music. My teacher got hold of some music by the German Wagner. His new opera, *Lohengrin*,[168] is very romantic, but I doubt if the opera ever makes it to far away San Francisco.

The Presidio officers are planning a ball. I will attend with my parents, and will let you know all about it in my next letter.

Stay well,

Burgundia

---

166 Flank steak is pounded flat. Each "bird" is layered with a mixture of chopped parsley, basil, garlic, olive oil, and salt pork. The "bird" is then rolled as per a jelly roll, and securely tied. The secret lies in the salt pork.

167 The precursor to the piano. The pianoforte or fortepiano—take your pick—has leather-covered hammers and harpsichord-like strings.

168 The most popular and recognizable part of the opera is the Bridal Chorus, better known as "Here Comes the Bride," often played as a processional at weddings.

25

Indian Friends

"When reaction takes place," said Doc, "it is best to stand from under."

"Meaning what?" I asked.

Billy added: "You're always talking in riddles."

"One man's riddle is another man's pearl of wisdom," Doc said. "My meaning is this, and, Billy, if I talk too fast please let me know. I recommend that we leave post haste. These Yankees are a flint-nose lot. Stealing is considered shrewdness, and outright swindling is only reckoned a sharp business transaction. Word's going to get out on what happened in the Trading Post. That lot is as full of mischief as a company of monkeys."

"They won't bother," said Billy. "Wasn't a man among them. And besides, we've got more friendly Injuns in our camp than old Montezuma had."

"Fat good that did him," I said.

Doc was insistent.... "I smell trouble and I counsel a quick exit. Those so-called friendly Indians are only waiting around for a free meal."

"Gassing won't get the job done," I said.

Within four hours we were on the road, aided by a rising moon and two dozen new Indian friends, puzzled no doubt that the dinner bell was not sounded that evening.

By first light our spirits were soaring. For the first time in our entire trip the young ladies were singing, harmonizing song after song to the delight of the Indians who murmured their approval at the end of each tune.

"This is the best day the world has ever seen," Doc sang out in full voice. Rick uncharacteristically added a second line: "Tomorrow will be better."

From a naked rise we watched the rosy light of dawn fill the great valley lying at our backs. When the gold mania leaves us, I recall thinking at that moment, that valley floor will be filled with planted fields and orchards, farm houses and the lowing herds of beef cattle and milk cows.

We paused to rest our blowing animals, and to cook up some burnt and ground coffee. The delights of sipping the decoction of the "brown berry" were not for our Indian friends, who giggled and made faces at the aroma of this strange new marvel of the white man.

The young ladies were a fascination to the Indians. This complicated a routine made necessary by outdoor travel in mixed company: the call of nature was answered by the ladies in whatever convenient bush presented itself to starboard; the men sought privacy to port. With Indians all about, our courtesans could not walk two paces in any direction without two or three or four escorts—and no amount of sign language and shouted orders to retreat could make the Indians understand.

Finally Opal took the lead. She retrieved a chamber pot from beneath a jumble of articles in the wagonette, sat it on the ground, hiked up her skirt, and sat down on the pot. "Me fill," she shouted, "'pppsssssssssssssssstttttt,' Me throw away! Woman—*osa*—this way; Man—*naña*—this way."

The white man's lust for gold will doom the Miwok Indians whose ancestral home for hundreds of year unfortunately for them nearly delineates the Sierra Nevada foothill gold regions—known as the Mother Lode.[169] I have lived sufficient years to see the Indian practically disappear from the California soil—a whole race of peaceful souls obliterated by disease and an occasional posse bent on lynching a human being for stealing a calf. These people were innocent of out hard-edged ways. Possession was not a sacred right. They did not understand how a man could own something that was alive as was the earth.

---

[169] The Miwok numbered about 8000. In the space of one year following the discovery of gold, an estimated 100,000 "aliens" from another world descended on them. It is tantamount today (1912) to San Francisco's population of 425,000 climbing to 55,600,000 in a year's time. And these newcomers all had firearms.

26

Sonoran Camp (1)

When we were a few miles out of Sonoran Camp, we side-tracked our outfit into an oak grove on Woods Creek, and Rick, Billy, and I beat it into town at railroad speed.

"All the States people are slow," said Billy. "Let them come out here to see a little life."

Sonoran Camp, as its name implies, was a Mexican settlement built into a mountain bowl. The town, because of its setting, had mostly crooked streets and dog paths. The early November nights were cold. Several wood choppers made a living supplying oak fuel wood, and through their effort the bowl the town sat in had a pleasant woodsy odor.

There were here at this time an incredible 10,000 Sonorans—expert placer miners and rabid gamblers, but the winds of change were also in the woodsy air: the Yankees would have this place and its gold for, the reasoning went, "We beat them fair and square in the war."

In the meantime—at the time we arrived—this was quite a city of noises, tents, booths, and log cabins; hotels, restaurants and businesses of all descriptions; canvas and cotton twill lean-tos; corrals of unhewn sticks with green branches and leaves and vines interwoven; people singing, yelling, fighting; doors and walls decorated with gaudy hangings of silks, fancy cottons, flags, many-tinted Mexican *zarapes*, the rich *manga* with its gold embroidery, Chinese scarfs and shawls of the most costly quality; horsemen, peons, tobacconists, spice merchants; gold and silver plated saddles, bridles, spurs;

wash tubs, basins; garbage, flies; drunks, gamblers, bakers, butchers, miners; freshly washed clothes, towels, rags hanging out to dry; women.

Sonora was probably the only place in the gold region where numbers of women were to be found. The Mexicans had brought their families, constructed brush huts for their women and children, and spread out looking for gold. There were not as yet any "white" women, that is, "American women." This fact, Hyrum Milton had told the young women in preparation for their relocation, would "insure your fortune."

The Sonorans measured social status by the gradation of the skin color of their wives and companions: the *mestiza* was the child of a white father and an Indian mother, rather dark, but preferable to the *china-blanca* who had a white father and a mother whose father was an Indian and mother a Negro or *mulatto*. The *china-blanca* ranked above the *quintera*, who was perfectly white, but came from Negro blood through the *mulatto*. She was preferable to the *zambas*, *zamba-claras*, *china-oscuras*, and *india-mestizas*.

I felt then as I feel now that this system of classifying people by the accident of their birth is deplorable.

While on the subject of women, I will add here further observations.

The Frenchwoman proved to be rather stiff competition to our young ladies. There were several in Sonora. They concentrated at the Lansquenet[170] tables and the liquor bars. Handsome and beautifully dressed, they sold their liquor at the going rate, but their sexual favors always went nightly to the highest bidder. Thus, they were able to make more in one "hop" than our young women made in a 12-hour shift.

The Spanish women (from Spain—not Mexico) were strictly upper-class true adventurers. Rarely did one venture

---

[170] A card game similar to monte. The dealer puts up a certain amount which bettors cover. Two cards are turned up, one for the dealer and the other for the bettors. The dealer then turns up the remaining cards, one at a time, until one of the two stake cards is matched.

from San Francisco to the mining camps. Educated and urbane, they were haughty with every reason to be so.

"The Yankee feels he is of a superior race and shows it by shunning the darker-skinned people," said Dandelion in the midst of a Casa Del Mar/Monte unending debate: what degree of darkness should be allowed entry. The Negro was out. Lascars? Kanackers? Feejees?

It was a curious and interesting situation. The whore, looked down upon by society, needing a class of people for it to look down at.

"The dark-skinned always hanker for the women of their betters," said Mary Turtle-Eyes.

"What, then, the Mexican?" Daphne asked, steering the debate to some sort of resolution.

"Hell's Fire," said Opal. "All there are in Sonoran Camp are Mexicans. I'm still sore from the ride Joaquin's men gave us."

On that long-ago day of arrival, Rick and I had *negocios graves* in Sonora. Billy insisted on coming along, but he operated on the strict condition that he not speak.

We called on a Mr. Samuel Newton, loosely associated with Hyrum Milton in an number of speculative ventures, including, I surmised, the Vista Del Monte. We met a very cordial man (what other than cordial would an associate of Hyrum be?) of some 60 years. He was well groomed except for the tangle of white hair atop his head.

Without asking our preference for refreshment, a servant brought forth seemingly everything the kitchen possessed—hard liquor, wine, beer, fruit ades, biscuits, candied nuts, sugarplums, chocolates, pastillage, oysters, head cheese, cinnamon tea, black tea, green tea, Darjeeling tea, rooibos tea, chamomile tea....[171]

---

[171] It is no mystery to me why C.H. provides so lengthy—and so obviously not true—a list of refreshments, especially of teas. It is an 'inside-the-family-joke.' The intended target is C.H.'s niece who became an insufferable snob after attending various "finishing schools." She was an apt student and learned what to say and how to say it in various social

Mr. Newton was charged with selecting and purchasing the site for the lacquered Chinese pleasure dome. He said getting title to land was complicated because every square inch of Tuolumne County was held by mining claims. However, he had been successful in buying outright the claims for the land needed for our operation. We would have to closely monitor any foundation or landscape digging. "I hired a couple of fellows to dig two cesspits so your crew would have a place to go," explained Samuel Newton. "Damned if they didn't hit a thin quartz vein, and we had a God-damned gold rush on our hands. Good thing is they dug those cesspits so deep you'll never be able to fill them."

We moved the outfit in the middle of the night to avoid what likely would have been a parade of unparalleled magnitude, honoring our Fourth of July, Mexico's independence from Spanish rule, Christmas, New Years, California's impending statehood, moving the Vista Del Monte from Monterey to Sonora in less than 90 days, and the anniversary of the Professors teaching the young ladies how to properly cook refried beans. Billy and Doc (again) said we should have had the parade "at high noon to air our merchandise."

I vetoed the plan. The young ladies are not "merchandise."

Reconstructing the singular building drew large crowds of onlookers. They particularly admired the fact Dandelion and her crew worked alongside the men in doing the heavy work such as unloading the wagons and putting the parts in place.

Scarlet took over the care of our livestock, holding impromptu auctions when two or three men showed interest in a particular animal. We would no longer need these "hay-burners," but one would think Scarlet had raised each animal

situations. This was especially true when the young lady assumed the role of hostess. C.H. tells how it would go when he called: "She'd rush over and give me a kiss on the cheek and say how nice it was to see me again even if I'd seen her an half-hour before. After a few more rehearsed statements, she'd ask if I'd like a cup of tea. No matter how I answered—'yes,' 'certainly,' 'of course,' 'that would be nice,' I never once got a cup of tea."

she sold from colthood by the way she shed tears to see a friend of the trail leave us. The buyer received, in addition to an animal well-cared for, a lecture on how her boy friend[172] Rick would not like it if he learned the animal had been abused.

Saturdays and Sundays were special in Sonoran Camp. The entire town became a festival of lights. Besides the candles burning in numberless open doors and windows, the gamblers cleared a space on the ground, spread their variegated *zarapes*, place a lighted taper in each corner, and pour into the center whatever gold or silver he wanted to risk.

The stalls on either side of the "main street" were loaded with *dulces, tacos, enchiladas, carnicitas, tamales,* and a popular sweet plum drink chilled by snow hauled down to Sonora from higher up the foothills.[173]

The heavy gamblers displayed in the center of their rich scarlet gold-embroidered zarapes banks of perhaps a thousand ounces, in silver dollars, gold doubloons, or small bags of gold dust. Coin demanded a premium of perhaps 20 percent, as coin was handy for gambling purposes by speeding up the process.

The gambler, like the whore, had only a narrow path of rectitude or virtue open to him. He was always descending, continually sinking in the slough of degradation. His very occupation made him a pariah. Hyrum's epistles were adamant: we were not to engage in gambling of any sort. We were not even to buy a lottery ticket that purports to raise money for the most innocent and worthwhile cause.[174]

There was a frenzy in the young nation. American frontier

---

[172] Rick's elevated status did not go unnoticed by C.H.'s coterie.

[173] I'm afraid C.H. is fudging here. November in Sonora is cold. The average November temperature dips down to 38 degrees. And November is the start of the rainy season which will bring an annual average of over 30 inches. This combination of cold and wet caused most of the gold seekers to retreat from the diggings.

[174] Sonora's most pressing need was for a hospital — not the ordinary general hospital, but one that specialized in the treatment of poison oak.

religion was sweeping west like a prairie fire. The Mormons were building Zion on the other side of the Sierras. The evangelists were thumping through the countryside selling salvation. The publishing houses were spewing long, dry tracts explaining what Jeremiah, Hosea, Zephaniah, and Malachi *really* meant. Religions were being organized, fractionalized, re-joined, re-dedicated. The times demanded a militant stance on all things, especially on the serious matter of the saving of one's immortal soul.

Many a dedicated Bible scholar tried to gain a foothold in Sonoran Camp. It would have been easier for a snowball to survive a summer in Hell. The citizens seemed happy and in no need to be preached out of that state of being.

I have, alas, wandered again. But, I approach the end of my "curious enterprise" and am reluctant to put down my pen. I little care if critics destroy this narrative, if 99 out of 100 who read these words spit it out after a bite or two. I want that 1 of 100 to pause and celebrate the life you have and the life I had. The only way we can speak from the grave is by what we write.

In so far as religion goes (the subject I started off with), I have a problem with Christianity (I no doubt would have a problem with the other religions if I had been exposed to them). Why, for instance should the son of god be complimented on being the son of David, an unmitigated adulterer? How could any civilized person believe in a god who would condemn his creatures to everlasting hell? Jesus preached to the wretched, advising them to be poor, to combat and extinguish nature, hate pleasure, seek suffering, and despise themselves? He tells them to leave father, mother, and all tied to life, in order to follow him.

I especially care not an iota what another person's "religion" might be. If he has a good heart, he can worship a shoe for all I care.

27

Sonoran Camp (2)

The miners prided themselves in meting out swift justice to those who were enemies of fairness and the general peace. Those of Mexican, South American, Eastern European, Mediterranean, or American Indian heritage also were dealt with swiftly, but seldom with justice. The Oriental had no rights whatsoever.

The lynch law was the supreme law of the land. It worked very well, erring no more than the justice of our day. And, of course, the '49er brand of justice was far cheaper to administer.

The California Supreme Court[175] had an uncanny ability to name as the chairman of its special lynching investigating committee (a different committee for each lynching) the very fellow who tied the noose around the unhappy victim's neck.

It was not uncommon to read in an official report that the case was dismissed because the "defendant was taken out and hanged by the mob."

Sonoran Camp was a-bust with red-shirted Anglos. The Mexican origins of the community were disappearing. Walking down the main strip one day we were treated to a vestige of a Mexican custom worth recounting here: the funeral procession of about a hundred men, women, and children.

"How's that for an omen," Billy said, a reference to a few minor problems we were experiencing at the Vista Del Monte

---

[175] The court came into existence when California was given statehood, which is a year or so in the future of his narrative at this point.

building site.

"Pay no heed," said Doc. "I've seen many Mexican funerals, and they appear to be happy affairs."

Happy affairs! Life in these put-together frontier towns was a hard dose to swallow without some sweetening.

The procession was led by six young girls dressed in white and bearing upon their shoulders the rough open coffin of an infant. On one side were two musicians, guitar and violin, playing such tunes as are heard in the country dances. On the other side were two fellows with ancient muskets, continually loading and firing into the air. Taking up the rear were a rambunctious group of boys setting off Chinese firecrackers which they exploded by the pack, making sure to make their fellow mourners or an occasional onlooker "dance and hop" to avoid the explosives thrown at their feet.

The grievers marched up to the cemetery, the coffin precariously placed alongside the freshly dug grave. As there were no flowers available at this time of year, carefully chosen sprigs of vegetation were strewn on the tiny body. And as there was no priest to officially send the dearly departed to a friendlier place than Sonoran Camp, the musicians, musketeers, and firecracker wielders continued until it was time to eat and dance. All departed for the home of the grieving parents where a grand *fandango* and feast took place, lasting throughout the night. The Musketeers ran out of black powder, the firecrackers were gone, but the music made it to dawn when a neighbor cried out, "*Maldita sea! Podemos a tener un poco de paz?*"[176]

As the Vista Del Monte project was nearing completion, our young women, stirred by some domicile instinct, festooned their friendly and familiar home with Christmas garlands, bunting, and branches of red berries.

There had been several letters from Burgundia, not exactly filled with promise and affection, but I concluded I expected too much. I was anxious to begin a new chapter in my life — hopefully with Burgundia, but if that was not to be, a new life nonetheless. We are always looking into the future, but all we see is the past.

Only youth is tolerable because great expectations are better than poor possessions.[177]

---

[176] *"God damn it! Can we have a little peace?"*
[177] Cervantes.

28

A Summons from Hyrum

A summons from Hyrum: "Meet me in Stockton at the port at noon, November 21. We are stopping there briefly on our way to Sacramento City. Bring Rick and Dandelion. Tell them to say only that I have asked to meet with you and that the three of you have no idea why—and actually you don't know why. You should bring invoices, receipts, etc. Dandelion should bring her books as well.

"P.S. We'll be having lunch at the fancy Golden Ledge. You three birds should dress accordingly."

Our early stage got into Stockton at 10, giving us two hours to speculate on Hyrum's intentions. We settled on the sale of Vista Del Monte. It would free him from the fear of disclosure. He could then pursue public service beyond his present role as a magistrate. Without the Vista Del Monte albatross hanging around his neck he could devote more time to making money.[178]

Hyrum's "we" turned out to be Luigi Crespi, the chef/proprietor of the Bay Side eatery. Burgundia had wanted

---

[178] C.H. said it was easy to become rich. All one had to do is devote every waking hour to the pursuit of riches, forsaking spouse, children, and family and—if any exist—friends. The recipe calls for the fortune-seeker to never spend money to accumulate memories, such as one gains through travel. C.H. traveled extensively. He and Burgundia saw all of Europe—England, Germany, France, Austria—London, Paris, Rome, Austria, Berlin, Potsdam, and Sans Souci. They sailed down the east coast of Africa. Business took him to Mexico, Chile, Alaska. He said so far as travel is concerned, his greatest regret was not having visited Iceland and its geysers.

to come, but obligations concerning an entertainment to be presented at the Presidio made it impossible. She was "coming along nicely" on the pianoforte.

A thriving restaurant in Sacramento City had fallen in Hyrum's hands, and Mr. Crespi might be able to remove the far-distance headache that particular business was giving him. "Except for Mr. Crespi here, I believe every chef on earth finds more passion in a dish of scrambled eggs than he does in an assignation with Venus di Milo," said Hyrum. Mr. Crespi blushed.

Hyrum was prepared to act on Rick Brazelton's petition — every bit of it news to both Dandelion and me — to collect his pay, Scarlet to cash out her earnings, the two of them to marry, the two of them, as husband and wife, to take up residency in San Francisco, and Mr. and Mrs. Rick Brazelton to cash in on Hyrum's "contract" to finance a suitable business venture at a more-than-generous rate of interest.

The news that Scarlet, like Persephone,[179] was to return to the respectable world, caused a genuinely joyful response from Dandelion. I, too, reacted to the good news by slapping Rick on the back, and asking, "When's all this going to happen?"

It happened in three days' time. Rick fetched Scarlet, returned to Stockton where they met Hyrum and Mr. Crespi on the return leg of their Sacramento City trip. Judge Hyrum married the couple.

Only the wedding witness, Mr. Crespi,[180] was in attendance.

---

[179] The daughter of Zeus and the harvest goddess Demeter, and queen of the Underworld whose annual return to the Aboveworld heralds the coming of Spring with the bursting-forth of vegetation. Rick and Scarlet aptly named their first child Persephone. Their second child, a boy, they named Hyrum. The Brazeltons owned and operated San Francisco's first flower shop.

[180] Mr. Crespi's wedding gift was a sumptuous feast attended by the Milton family.

29

Zachary Fenner's Bees

Ambition has no rest.

"Sonora welcomed two distinguished visitors Friday as a premium for the success of their up and coming mountain metropolis. They are the Honorable Zachary Fenner, a distinguished San Francisco attorney and delegate to the late California Constitutional Convention, and the Very Reverend Dr. John Cowan, newly appointed Vicar of the Interior and Southern California Divisions of the Church of the Savior.

"The gentlemen are put up in the Gunn House[181] where they daily comment favorably on their 'first class' accommodations and the bright prospects of our city.

"The distinguished clergyman is a handsome specimen of manhood in the prime and vigor of his life, well-formed, with florid complexion, gray hair and whiskers.

"Mr. Fenner, a veteran of the War with Mexico, is rumored to be a strong candidate to challenge politicians on the state level, having made important friends in Monterey, San José, San Francisco, Benicia, Sacramento City and now in Sonora—'Queen of the Southern Mines.'"

Here I was reminded of the favorite quotation of my Latin Teacher in Boston: *Quot ignavi gerere super mento barbae*

---

[181] Here again C.H.'s chronology is off. We are entering December, 1849, in his narrative and the Gunn House was not constructed until the following year. Dr. Lewis C. Gunn of Philadelphia was the original owner, and that same Lewis Gunn published the Mother Lode's first newspaper, the *Sonora Herald*. The flowery description of Fenner and Cowan's visit is taken from that newspaper.

Hercules?[182]

"The Rev. Cowan graduated with first honors from Columbia College, New York, and delivered a Greek salutary oration on that occasion. His fame achieved as a Monterey preacher is too well known to take the reader's time to recount. The emphasis of his Tuolumne crusade will be to 'shine the cleansing light of truth on the damnable practice of prostitution.' In Monterey he is credited with the purification of the former capital of California by the forcing out of the notorious Vista Del Mar house of ill repute. That den of inequity has been resurrected in Sonora as the Vista Del Monte, the red and yellow lacquered Chinese house that now dominates the once pure 'vista' of God's mountains.

"The famed churchman and his equally famous traveling companion have promised to spend a fortnight in Sonora, and all are welcome to present to them petitions before the dinner hour at the Gunn House.

"On Sunday next the Rev. Cowan will preach in the Columbia meeting hall in the former premises of the Cheap for Cash Store. He has chosen for his topic temperance: 'Bacchus has drowned more men than has Neptune. A drunkard qualifies for all vices.' The Columbia Daughters of Temperance will serve refreshments following the sermon.

"On the Friday following, at sunset, the two distinguished visitors will lead a torch-light parade to the grounds of the Vista Del Monte where Rev. Cowan will present his final address. He has taken for his sermon topic the words of St. Matthew (iii.4) 'Raiment of camel's hair, and a leathern girdle about his loins; and his meat was locusts and wild honey.'"

This was a fire bell sounding in the night. Rick's absence compounded my problem.

I called immediately on Samuel Newton, our first contact in Sonora. I caught him while he was on his way, newspaper clutched in his hand, to see me. Hyrum had to have this

---

[182] "How many cowards wear on their chins the beard of Hercules?"

intelligence. Newton said he would himself take it to him in San Francisco — if indeed Hyrum was at home. What happened to the sealed indictment against Fenner? Did the San Francisco Presidio have rapid access to the Monterey officers, Martin Hayes and James Whiteside? In the meantime I would mobilize our defenses. How this would be done I had not the slightest clue.

Gloom permeated the kitchen where the entire crew met to explore options. There was one: watch the Vista Del Monte go up in flames. "Lacquer burns real good," said Billy.

"Any show of resistance will give Fenner the excuse to riot," I said, "and with the rioting will come the torches."

"Even at Christmas time we are not to be spared," said Mary Turtle-Eyes. All the young ladies save Dandelion were sniffling.

Besides the Vista crew there were in the kitchen a pair of *perros mascoti* — "pet dogs" — the "regulars" who concentrate their social and sexual attention on a single girl. One of these was a woodsman-turned-successful-miner named Fred Adolphos, Dandelion's *perro*.

Fred had an idea. He read the last part of the sermon topic aloud: "...and his meat was locusts and wild honey." Then added: "There's our answer."

With the help of Fred's knowledge of the workings of nature, and divine providence, we defeated Fenner and Cowan. We saved the Vista Del Monte, and by some miracle our whorehouse became the object of veneration by some devout folk who apparently went in for this sort of thing.

Here's how we did it.

Gertie the seamstress was given the task of sewing together eight canvas bags of a specific shape and size.

Phiggy the watchmaker was given the task of fashioning sixteen mesh screens of a specific shape and size.

Billy the sailor was given the task of braiding eight ropes of a specific length.

The Professor — the *majordomo* — was given the task of visiting all the Mexican *tiendas* and purchasing all the honey, jams, and jellies he could lay his hands on.

Doc, Opal, Mary Turtle-Eyes, and her *perro* Robert Flint were given the task of following Fred into the woods.

We let it be known that because of the rally the Vista Del Monte would not be doing business that day.

The scouts—Doc, Opal, Mary Turtle-Eyes—had marked eight huge beehives, their occupants sleeping away the cold nights.

Phiggy had fashioned ventilator grills which Gertie had sewn into her canvas bags that resembled overstuffed Dutch pillows.

The hives were dropped into the bags which were quickly sealed.

Meanwhile, back at the Vista Del Monte, the Professor and his helpers rearranged the boulders that defined the long path to the building, making that path narrower.

The young ladies boiled the honey and other sweets so the concoction could be "painted" on the entry boulders and shrubbery.

Fred marshaled the Vista Del Monte troops to keep the bees, slowly recovering from their uprooting, cool by vigorous fanning.

The Professor, Doc, Phiggy, and Robert Flint stationed themselves at the base of the road, turning away gawkers and customers who had not heard the news about being closed.

An hour before the sun was to set, the bee bags were gingerly placed out of sight, four on each side of the honey-smeared path boulders. Billy attached the trigger ropes with the precision and caution of a sapper about to end the war by blowing up the enemy's castle. A slight tug by Billy hidden on one side of the path, and by Daphne on the other, and the war would be over! "Don't forget to get the hell out of there," were Billy's last instructions to Daphne.

Fenner had hired the two-piece Mexican band, and had even supplied the hard-to-manage firecracker brigade with more firepower that they had ever seen at one time.

The parade was forming. The martial band was tuning up. There were many feminine voices drifting up the street. I was hoping women and children would be spared the bee stings about to be inflicted on them.

Then an idea struck me. "Doc," I said, "come with me. I'm going to tell Fenner we will fight them if they step foot on our property."

"What good will that do?" asked Billy.

"It'll force them to put their women and children to the rear."

"If I know Fenner," said the Professor in a rare comment to the entire group, "that son-of-a-bitch will shove them ahead."

We had overlooked the need for a signal to let the bees out of the sacks.

Doc came through. As soon as Fenner, waving his torch, was three-fourths the way up our path and obviously confused because there were no defenders "ready to fight" as promised, Doc stepped out onto the front porch and proclaimed:

"Cry 'Havoc!' And let slip the bees of war!"

Whether it was the music or the firecrackers or the torches or the being awakened several months before time or the overpowering scent of nectar or each hive being flung into a world inhabited by seven other sets of foreigners, the bees were confused and murderously upset.

Fenner was so badly stung he required evacuation to San Francisco.

Rev. Cowman was also badly stung, but the taunts that followed him for his choice of a subject matter for his sermon—"his meat was locusts and wild honey"—stung him. God had favored the Vista Del Monte, gave it status—perhaps divine status at the expense of Cowan's lifelong crusade to stamp out evil. Why?

When Hyrum got the whole story, he sent me a bank draft of $1000 to present to Fred Adolphos "at an appropriate ceremony."

30

Life in Sonora

I found it strange that during his two weeks in Sonora, Rev. Cowan apparently had made no attempt to contact Billy Tremaine who was, after all, an eligible suitor for his daughter. And, even if that did not work out the preacher and the millionaire and their families had much in common, including an exaggerated opinion of how high on the social ladder they perched.

The only real work left on Vista Del Monte was the landscaping, and after that was finished Billy would be superfluous. (And, come to think of it, so would I.)

Unless...Billy, who had no desire to leave Vista Del Mar and Daphne (whose "volume" was on a steady decline—this information volunteered by Dandelion) for the all-consuming embrace of Uncle Phineas's thriving business and the suffocating embrace of the Cowan's daughter Hope....

Unless...Hyrum decides Billy is the ideal sort to help run a whorehouse, and I am not. At least I hope I am not.

The two parolees, Doc and Phiggy, would find their way in the gold country. So far Hyrum had not indicated when they should be terminated—or even if they were to be let go. Hyrum was always juggling a dozen balls at a time, thus always in need of trustworthy men to fill key assignments.

Upon reflecting on the "no fraternizing" rule I abandoned, there were both good and potentially very bad outcomes. The good, of course was Rick and Scarlet. The wait-and-see good is the Opal and Doc pairing: a potentially jarring union of two strong characters. It would be interesting

The I-only-see-trouble-ahead couple is Billy and Daphne. He is headstrong, she a romantic. As soon as he grows up and accepts the opportunity thrust upon him by his uncle, Daphne will melt into the obscurity of an unmarked whore's grave.

There was a definite mood shift in the Vista following our victory over the forces of misdirected righteousness. All were more relaxed, open to honest discussion, a feeling of friendship, and humor.

Doc, as usual, had the right words: "For a time there, caught as we were between a supposed man of God and a God-awful man, I felt like a fish between two cats."

"Speaking of cats," said Opal, "We were lucky that Dandelion's pussy still held some attraction for Fred the Bee Man." A new Dandelion led the laughter.

"One thing is certain," said Daphne, "The Vista Del Monte has made its last move. There can be no profit in allowing Rev. Cowan to chase us up and down the length and breadth of California."

"Amen," said Opal.

Meanwhile business at the Vista Del Monte — known to our Mexican neighbors as *casa de las abejas* — "House of the Bees" — was booming. Winter had driven the placer miners to warmer quarters. Some companies attempting to divert water from streams to expose the rich river and creek beds had to give up until more favorable conditions returned. Wintertime Sonora was filled with unattached men.

Our young ladies had no real competition, even from sweethearts and especially from wives. And while the Mexican might suffer an Anglo to put a foot onto his mining claim, he did not tolerate even a long glance at his wife or daughter.

The few French and Spanish adventuresses went to the highest bidder, and usually the highest bidder was the same man night after night, stretching into weeks and sometimes months until the transfer of his fortune to her account was complete.

The Anglo miners were a rough bunch. Drifters, irregulars, dreamers, malcontents, some wanted by the law, were not squeamish about patronizing a sporting house. Ninety-five of every one-hundred miners considered themselves fortunate to make wages. Turning ground and hauling water to wash it is hard work, make no mistake of it. The miners averaged but a dollar a day, small pay when one considers miserable New England rum sold for a quarter-dollar per shot glass.

When the heavy rains came and the freight wagons from Stockton had to be put up, the prices went even higher. The young ladies kept the lid on their price: two dollars. Their business was not touched by the weather.

The miners had few means to combat monotony—foot races and dog fights being the favorites. Big stakes were placed on runners. Because a fast runner could not be absolutely certain of victory—but could be of defeat—it was not unheard of for a runner to slip in a bet on an opponent. The trouble begins, of course, when both runners use this technique. I witnessed such a race in my first week in Sonora. The enraged miners broke the legs of both runners.

There is a spirit of emulation among miners which prevents them from being satisfied with success while others around them are more successful. Thus it is that if one miner hears, for example, that Princess is heaven-come-to-earth, he'd be quick to give her a try. When another miner gets word that Gertie is more lovely than the loveliest, he'll shuck his steady—probably Princess—and move in on Gertie.

I am guilty in these jottings of giving the young women an aura almost of saintliness, of victims of cruel circumstance. Believe me when I say they were far from being models of piousness. There were bouts of petty jealousy. The sexual act, even when paid for, at various and unexpected times may elicit a spiritual bond between the two participants. If the young man mounted between the whore's legs is imagined by her to be some reincarnation of a lad she loved in her innocent days, the mind goes along with the pretense. So when that young man returns and in examining the merchandise passes up our delusional lass and choses another, the shattered romance leads to ill feelings at best and violence at worst.

In my short time at the Vista I witnessed several fights—usually hair-pulling—between the young women. These storms usually passed quickly.

As the days stretched past our first Christmas and the New Year, it became evident that the Vista Del Monte was secure and even welcomed in Sonora (the "Camp" was no longer used).

Our two parolees, Phiggy and Doc, were let go with enough wages in their pockets to give them a start in San Francisco. Gertie gave Phiggy an affectionate kiss, and Opal did the same with Doc, and all ties were thus severed.[183]

That left six young ladies and Billy, the Professor, me, and an important new member of our coterie—Dandelion's *perro*, the Hero of the Battle of the Bees, Fred Adolphos.

The Professor continued as the "outside man," and Billy took over Rick's job as the "inside man." And Fred filled in where needed, which usually was the kitchen. I had nothing to do or say about the business taking place in the lacquered Chinese palace, nor did I have pay or profit from it. In fact, I had had no pay as yet from Hyrum, recalling that our "contract" called for me to receive a portion of the money gained through the sale of the building. But, when was that

---

[183] All four of these characters had "happy endings." Gertie married a Russian who struck it rich with the discovery of the Burning Moscow Mine in the Southern California desert. Opal quit the "business" and married a miner who made a big strike on the Trinity River in far northern California. Doc returned, briefly, to the practice of phrenology and when he ran out of cranial San Francisco bumps to read returned to his home in Connecticut. Phiggy went into the jewelry business in San Francisco.

going to be? And was I stuck here in Sonora with nothing to do but wait for Samuel Newton to come running up the hill dragging behind him a prospective buyer?

Dandelion tolerated no tom-foolery amongst her paying guests. She slapped one old boy newly out of the woods for running a hand up her skirt. He cursed her and went for her, but Fred stepped out of the kitchen and nearly drove him through the lacquered partition.

The chief complaint the young women had concerning their customers had to do with the personal habits of these men fresh from the wilderness.

My "chief complaint" I outlined above: it was time to leave the wilderness of Sonora. All this I wrote to Hyrum. His response was curt: "Meet us at the Stockton pier at noon the 23rd. I'd like to meet Mr. Adolphus."

"Us?"

Another business exploration with Mr. Crespi?

Or Burgundia?

31

Burgundia

Hyrum and Burgundia were on the river steamer's prow. I'll never forget the ship's name: *Confidence*.

Soon as we made visual contact, Hyrum left the scene. Fred did likewise.

It was Burgundia and me.

We had between us one night of passion—one.

I had to ask: "Have you forgiven me?"

"All I think about is you," she said. "I should have let you do it so you'd know how much I love you," then added: "Do you think me awful for saying that?"

"I think you're wonderful," I said.

A discreet clearing of his throat told us Hyrum Milton had joined us. Burgundia remained in my arms and kissed me full on the lips in the presence of her father, who merely patted both of us on our heads to tell us it was time to have lunch—again at the Golden Ledge which proudly announced it was under new management: Hyrum now owned controlling interest.

The essence of my conversation with Hyrum was: He wanted me to stay with the Vista Del Monte six to eight more weeks, through the winter. From the intelligence he gathered (from Rick and Scarlet? from Dandelion? from spies? from Samuel Newton?) Billy was not the answer to the Vista Del Monte's top mail *honcho*. "Going back to Monterey should not be that difficult for an impoverished sailor. There's something amiss here."

Fred Adolphos, perhaps by way of paying for his lunch, offered some insight: "When we were about to unleash our bees, Caesar here had a pang of the humanitarian. He did not want women and children to be stung. By a clever ruse they were situated mostly out of harm's way. When the bees were doing their intended work those of us at the windows were stung—pardon the pun—by the great pain we were inflicting on our fellow citizens. There were no celebratory cries from our side—except from the person you are discussing. Billy Boy was urging on the bees."

32

Civic Violence

In the weeks that followed our meeting, there was a strange falling off of correspondence from Burgundia. A note about a new song learned on the pianoforte, some social doings at the Presidio. For my part my letters were getting fusty for lack of any news not touching on the young ladies, who were making plenty of news.

Princess and Mary Turtle-Eyes, taking a morning constitutional, found a scurvy victim in a snowdrift and brought him back to the Vista. Scurvy was rampant among the miners, the result of a lack of vegetables and vegetable acids. The first symptom is a swelling and bleeding of the gums followed by swelling of both legs below the knees. This was not, of course, reported in the *Sonora Herald*.

Because of the extreme intimacy of the work they do, the Vista Del Monte young ladies follow a strict protocol concerning health matters, starting with a search for abnormalities in the mouth, the face and hands of the fully clothed client. This is followed by a thorough examination and washing of the male genitalia. If, however, there is any sign of an infection, the young ladies excused themselves from the room on the pretext of having forgotten something. They returned with an escort and the customer's money, a bar of robust hand soap, and a broadside with information on the best hygienic practices.

I'm sure Burgundia would have welcomed this sort of (light) discourse.

Even with the threat of a couple more winter storms, the armies of men preparing to invade the diggings were assembling: cheerful, healthy, cocky. Their apparel a universal uniform: a pair of overalls and a red check shirt, sturdy boots. They share a common desire: to get rich and then return home. The bitter truth is come October this same army will retreat, its foot soldiers victims of fever and ague, sallow, weak, emaciated, dispirited.

They were young, homesick, sentimental. In two year's time there would be 100,000 of them in a 20 x 60-mile enclave. During the peak of activity they would take out $80,000,000 in gold, much of it lying atop the ground ready for easy picking, and then, for all practical purposes, the rush for gold would be over. The easy bits and pieces — the "low-lying fruit" — was gone. From that point forward, it would be a business — a job like the one in the East they turned their back to.

Along with their dreams the newcomers brought with them many strange machines.[184] They came in every imaginable shape and size — all resembling bizarre appliances from a peopled moon. The one thing these various machines had in common is that they all failed in the work of separating gold from gaff. They were abandoned in favor of the tried and true "rocker," which receives ore at one end and collects the gold on its riffles at the other.

A man can make a living in these hills with a sheath-knife and a crow-bar to work the rock crevices. One old miner, a "steady" at the Vista, became more excited discussing gold than he did at a "Men in the Vista" lineup. He contended that even upon the rivers' banks the very earth has been thrown aside as useless, but even that which has been once washed, will still, with careful washing in a pan, turn out three to ten dollars per day. Dream on....

Throughout the range of the western Sierra and in every

---

[184] Most of these machines came by ship at considerable freight cost. Some mining companies even shipped steel safes to hold their loot.

little hill that branches from it, runs a formation of quartz rock, sometimes found on the surface, sometimes hundreds of feet below the earth's surface, and sometimes arising above it in a huge solid mass. This quartz is richly impregnated with gold. Huge costly machines are needed to extract this quartz, to crush it in stamp mills. The economics involved require a thousand bushels of crushed quartz rock must be produced each day.

The "old timer" — probably not yet 50 years of age: California was a young man's kingdom — quoted above made and spent three small fortunes with his sheath-knife and crow-bar. He was one of thousands who passed through. Each had a story to tell[185] — or in the case of James Marshall, discoverer of

---

[185] C.H., despite an occasional puncturing of the dreams of the young men who came to California, has high praise for the Gold Rushers and their stories. It was a Christmas ritual for him to tell the story of Ben Yorty, a young miner who followed the lure of easy riches to the Mother Lode, then over the Sierra to the Comstock, and finally south to the Mojave Desert. Yorty was a loner. He kept to himself. ¶ Yorty set up a camp in Cantil and quickly realized he would need a pack animal if he was going to penetrate the away country. The owner of the local corral had a couple of mules, six burros, and a White Horse for sale. Yorty bought the White Horse. The other prospectors knew, of course, the utter stupidity of prospecting the desert with a horse. It had to do with water, or more precisely the lack of water. A horse needed five times the amount of water than did a burro, a fact his fellow campmates never failed to remind him of. ¶ The prospectors' important source of income came from guiding rich dilettantes into the deep recesses of the desert — a trade in which Yorty could not participate. Once, while he lay ill with a fever, the daughter of the owner of the general store took care of the White Horse, which she had admired — but secretly so as not to be the target of derision from the local wags. By way of thanking the girl, Yorty tried to give her a brooch that had been his mother's. The girl's response was to redden and refuse the gift which might be mistaken for some sort of token linking the prospector with the White Horse and the girl in the general store. ¶ But, there was something between them. When the boys were snorting over the latest White Horse caper, she uncharacteristically asked them if they didn't have something better to talk about. The next day the White Horse was gone. It took Yorty a fortnight to track down the White Horse. When he returned to camp some of his fellow prospectors, whether through shame or guilt, welcomed him home. ¶ The daughter of the general store owner kept a confidence buried deep within

the nuggets in John Sutter's sawmill trace that launched the gold rush of California — history's first truly international race for riches.

Sunday night was the slowest in the business week. The miners kept the Sabbath in practically all things. Most tried to honor the commitment made to a devout mother. Sundays

---

her soul: she was sweet on Yorty. But she strove to keep that secret stillborn because, as was common knowledge throughout the vast stretches of the Mojave Desert, the man with the White Horse was deranged — not violently so, but strangely so. While Yorty chose to squander away material treasure by ridiculously keeping a water-guzzling White Horse, she was determined not to squander away her treasure — her virginity — on this good man's one deep blemish. Yet, she was drawn to him and he to her. ¶ The girl's father sensed a bad stew was cooking in his very kitchen, so when an offer came to buy his business his daughter's situation firmed up his mind. He traded the general store for — of all things — a small horse ranch in the Tehachapi Mountains. It only took two months for the father to realize the utter isolation of their new home was exactly what a young girl did not need by way of being "rescued." ¶ The father relented. "Send word to Yorty that we have some work he can do at our horse ranch," the father said to his daughter. "I already have," said the girl. ¶ One of the most persistent myths regarding the desert is that man and beast become acclimated to summer heat. The blood "thins out." The opposite is true: the summers become increasingly harder to take. When the White Horse's signs of weakening steadily increased, Yorty no longer took the White Horse on his jaunts. Unfortunately the girl's invitation came in scorching mid-August. Man and horse traveled at night. They climbed the foothills forming the eastern base of the Tehachapis. The road pitched sharply upward. The White Horse was heaving great droughts of breath. It several times slipped. Some passing prospectors advised Yorty to shoot the animal to release it from its misery. "We're nearly home," Yorty told them. ¶ And, indeed, after providing the White Horse with a sunshade of vegetation and what was left of their water, the night that followed found them at the girl's horse ranch. ¶ The White Horse died of exhaustion. The girl's father suggested that they butcher the carcass and feed it to the hogs. The girl would have none of it. "We'll bury the White Horse here," she said. Yorty, the girl, and her father went to work digging a trench alongside the White Horse. When it was deep enough they planned to roll the White Horse into it. ¶ The digging became increasingly difficult mainly because they had uncovered a quartz vein which did not seem to have a bottom to it. In fact it did not have a bottom that they would ever reach. The quartz was shot through with gold filigree and egg-sized nuggets. This discovery would be the named the White Horse Mine.

were for quiet contemplation, for washing clothes, gathering firewood, reading scripture, or for recovering from Saturday night's ruinous interest in rum and whiskey — but, for most, definitely not a day for whoring.

We lingered over the remains of the spent meal in our cozy kitchen. While the three younger girls were entertaining customers, Gertie, Opal, and Dandelion were chortling over a bit of sewing. If women lost us Eden, such as she alone restored it.

Suddenly there came the sound of great commotion from down the hallway. Princess's door flew open and she emerged screaming,

We leaped to our feet and pushed into the hall. Princess was bleeding about her neck and shoulder. The women quickly gathered her into the kitchen.

Her assailant was upon us.

Hairy and naked except for his boots, he too was bleeding. A piece of his outer ear dangled apart from the rest of the ear.

We knew him by the name "Hog," an infrequent visitor.

It so happened that the Professor was first in line; further it so happened he had been called from his kitchen work of cutting up a carcass of venison, which meant he was armed with a large, wicked, sharp, slicing knife.

All the while, in an instance, Daphne and Mary Turtle-Eyes and John Doe-1 and John Doe-2 decanted into the hallway in the ultimate demonstration of *coitus interruptus*.

Hog, enraged, raised his hairy fist to smash us all; the Professor, likewise infuriated by instinct, reached back over the centuries to call on the wisdom of his ancestors, a knife-savvy tribe of survivors. *Tio* Plano had schooled him on how to repel a grizzly bear about to kill you in a bear hug — to wit: hold your knife handle with two hands against your sternum, the blade pointing away. Defense! Let the bear (or Hog) apply the strength, the aggressor hoist with his own petard.

The Professor calculated the trajectory of Hog's blow — in this case on the top of the Professor's head. The knife was placed, the blow delivered, the Hog hoisted with his own petard. He crashed through a lacquered wood panel and ran naked and screaming down the Path of the Bees to an otherwise peaceful Sonora Sabbath.[186]

Billy started to give chase, but I stopped him. "Get these boys out of here," I said, indicating the two customers. "Get them their clothes."

"Wait 'til I give them back their money," said Dandelion.

"Hell, keep the money," said one of the Doe's. "A good stabbin' beats a poke any time."

The others were ministering to the hysterical Princess. When she calmed down we got the story. The blood was not hers — and neither was it Hog's! She bit his ear, alright, but only after he killed a pigeon and smeared its blood on Princess while he was climaxing — a bit of depravity imported from San Francisco's Barbary Coast.

"Better get the new sheriff up here," said the other Doe. "That fellow with the bit ear will cause you trouble. We'll take his stuff and give it to him. He shouldn't be hard to find."

---

[186] I can attest to the phenomenon of time "slowing down" as experienced by the Professor. In my late 30's I was inspecting a piece of mining machinery which featured an axle rapidly turned by a steam-powered flywheel. I was standing a foot from the whirling axle when I reached over it to adjust a valve. As I did so, a stray strand of wool from the sleeve of my sweater wrapped itself around the axle. And my sweater began unraveling — with me snugly trapped within it! My immediate thought was that my situation was dire, most likely fatal. But, the amazing thing is that time slowed down so I could examine my options: I could try to rip loose from the axle — no good; my shirt under the sweater is new, made of sturdy material, and buttoned at the wrist. I could let the machine take its course — at worse I would be mangled to death; at "best" my right arm would be yanked out of its socket. Or I could throw myself horizontally on the shaft — not enough room. Or I could bend over and try with my left hand to free my right arm by passing the garments over my head — the buttoned shirt wrists again. Now time was screaming into my very being. ACT! I stepped back, drove my chest against the shaft, then pulled back with all my might. My sweater and my new coarse shirt ripped down both sides as neatly as had I cut the fabric with a pair of tailor's shears.

"We'll tell the new sheriff straight what happened," said his partner.

Meanwhile the Sunday night vigil at the Baptist Church was about to begin. The new minister, Owen Lovejoy,[187] vastly misnamed, was a man of considerable brain and a good deal of body. Several men engaged him in hurried conversation at the pulpit.

Something was amiss.

Lovejoy's technique was to start his homily at the very top of his voice, which some characterized as a cannonade.

When he was about to transition from a boom to a roar, some wag at the back of the room called, "Louder!" The effect upon the congregation was paroxysmal.

Rev. Lovejoy got right to the point: "On yonder hill, claiming a site worthy of a cathedral of God, stands a heathen China-made house of prostitution, violence, and sin.

"I have just received word that one of your fellow Sonorans, while strolling on the public road that circles our city, was set upon not an hour ago by two brazen whores and their sexual procurers. The women robbed him of his clothes and his wallet, while one of the men, a Mexican, stabbed him in the ear and hand."

The man of God was not allowed to finish his fable.

The new sheriff stood at the door. "Pardon me," he said, gaining the floor. "I take my text from the Commandment, 'Thou shall not bear false witness.' The truth is the man named Hog was not robbed of his clothes. He removed them voluntarily—nay, it would be more accurate to say enthusiastically—at the Vista Del Monte. And, he was not stabbed—he stabbed himself."

"How do you know all what you say is true?" Rev. Lovejoy asked the new sheriff. "How does a man stab

---

[187] Rev. Lovejoy did not come to California until 1856. My guess is that C.H. could not pass up the joke about the man calling the bombastic preacher to speak "Louder."

himself?"

"The testimony comes from an unimpeachable source," the new sheriff said, "your nephews Albert and Thomas, who happened to be on a backwoods quail hunt where they were able to see the entire affair."

The new sheriff explained that Hog ran at Pablo Perez, who had drawn his knife for self-protection.

The new sheriff was Samuel Newton.

33

Daphne and Billy

It was evident that Daphne was having a rough time with her dead-end relationship with Billy. She was answering fewer and fewer "Men in the Parlor" calls. He seemed not to care whether she had intercourse with twenty men or no men on any given day. He demonstrated fondness for her company, but that had migrated from a playful relationship that truly appeared enjoyable for both of them, to one that appeared more serious, especially more anxious on her part.

Billy was Billy. He was easy-going, friendly, good-humored. It is said that the most successful lotharios are men who do not display seriousness. The earnest kind rob a girl of the few carefree months she will enjoy between adolescence and the eventual "duty" of marriage. The lighthearted swain does not threaten. He does not suffocate by taking charge. In fact, he is mostly not interested in taking charge.

The young ladies were none of my business unless something they did threatened the good name—that is, the Vista Del Monte's market value. My job was to protect the enterprise's worth until it could be sold. Hyrum was not interested in the whorehouse business; he was interested in parlaying the building itself into a tidy profit.

At our last meeting in Stockton I overheard him say to one of his business cronies that his portfolio was top-heavy with real estate holdings, and that soon he would need to convert "dirt into cash" because he had two unmarried daughters[188]

---

[188] Zinfandella never married. (See footnote 46)

likely "to run off with some penniless beggar, and it would be up to Daddy to pick up the pieces."

I was stunned by this disclosure. It put me on my guard. Hyrum had the power to have prevented Burgundia and me from ever having met, or to have been alone together in the same room. Yet, I had held her naked body. For all he knew I could have taken her virginity, all, seemingly, with his tacit approval or, at best, because of his inaction.

Meanwhile, Billy was making fewer and fewer trips into Stockton for hardware needed to complete the Vista Del Monte project—items like door knobs, kerosene lamps, trims, and furniture bumpers—little things that were miniscule compared to the orders purchased from his uncle's hardware store during the boom phase of the reconstruction project.

Phineas, who trusted nobody but himself with the company books, noticed this decline, and sent a letter to Billy via the Stockton store: "Your little adventure is over, time to come home and make your fortune." And P.S.: "don't forget to collect your wages."

Daphne was the last to learn of Billy's exit plans. He sloughed it off as a mere nothing; the inevitable consequence of their situation; there was nothing by way of work for him in Sonora, and he'd be damned if he was going to scratch for gold; he'd had enough of the hard life on the *Tronka*.

A whore's greatest sin is not the obvious: having sex for pay; it is falling in love. If that affection is not reciprocal, as it was with Scarlet and Rick, then the unloved partner will get a preview of the eternal hell she knows awaits her.

Daphne presented Dandelion with an unstable problem. At her urging I expedited Billy's departure, paying him off from the pot of money the young ladies had earned from their honest labors. (In my capacity as "project manager" I rarely handled cash.)

Two weeks later we learned from the Professor, who took over Billy's Stockton supply run, that Billy was the new manager of the Tremaine Stockton outlet, and the bans were posted for his marriage to Rev. John and Abigail Cowan's daughter, Hope.

This news was received by the Vista Del Monte's kitchen frequenters with caution. Daphne had walked to the edge of a yawning precipice—it was up to her to back away from the disaster it threatened.

She appeared cheerful and even joked with the clients in the "Men in the Parlor" line up. She even seemed to have picked up a "steady"—a stage driver.

Twenty days after Billy's departure, Daphne took the stage to Stockton and shot Billy in the neck.

Billy bled to death in the Tremaine Hardware Store's rat poison section.[189]

---

[189] C.H. does not tell Daphne's fate, nor was I able to find anything about her post-Billy in the public or private archives. Years after this incident I met a Yankee who was an eye-witness to the shooting. He said when Billy was sniveling for his life, Daphne commented that that was the first time she had ever seen him serious about anything to do with her. ¶ Billy's murder was an *escándalo por excelencia* in Monterey. The Tremaines became societal pariahs. It was rumored that Hope Cowan became insane, but, as a neighbor was quoted as saying, "How was one to tell?"

34

Fenner Turns Up in Sonora

With the winter rains behind us and the search for a *bona fide* buyer for the Chinese lacquered house formally announced, I was swimming in a sea of exuberance.

I walked into Sonora to buy an ounce of snuff, a fist-full of cheroots, and the latest outside newspaper I could lay hands on.

Standing at the tobacconist's canvas stall, I heard a familiar voice address me.

"Mr. Honore," said Zachary Fenner, "Fancy meeting you in this rough and muddy out-station."

"Mr. Fenner," I said, "as a 'rising star among politician'—I think that is how you were christened in one of the San Francisco rags—you should know it is not wise for 'a rising star' to degrade a community. These people are voters too."

"Well put, Mr. Honore," said my nemesis. "You are forever giving me lessons beneficial to me and my so-called career. While it appears we do not have much in common, I do apologize for striking flint to your powder every time we meet."

"I am as much to blame," I answered, always quick to be disarmed by a showing of civility.

"I don't suppose," he said, "now that your job is done that I could pry from you the name of the man who owns that remarkable Chinese structure?"

"I don't suppose," I said.

"I admire your loyalty," he said, "but the name will be

known as a matter of law as soon as the deed is transferred."

"Three thoughts on that point," I said. "First, from what I have seen of the law in my brief stay in California, the person with the deepest pockets writes the law, second, he interprets it, and then, if he chooses, ignores it."

Fenner smiled — for him a painful gesture that caused a passing dog to curl its upper lip in imitation.

"Honore," he said, dropping the 'Mr.', "Your patron is Hyrum Milton — the righteous and colorful judge who has achieved the stature of a 'living legend' in San Francisco. The very pious and high-minded public servant who aspires to rise to the heights of political power in San Francisco — in California — in the United States — who just happens to have a whorehouse shackled to his feet of clay."

"I'm sorry," I said, "I don't know the man."

"You certainly know his daughter, Burgundia," he said. "Two or three letters a week pass between you."

I was robbed of breath. It took all my concentration to reply: "Tampering with the mails again. You know that is a hanging offense."

"Alexander Todd's Jackass Express is not the U.S. Mail," Fenner said. Todd and his agents had toured the mines and registered the residents who wanted them to retrieve letters from the San Francisco post office. The subscribers paid the enterprising man two dollars per letter and four dollars per hometown newspaper delivered.

"From the letters I read," said Fenner in an evenness of tone that further unnerved me, "Burgundia confined her comments to school and pleasantries...."

Here I struck him full on the jaw. His legs gave way and he fell backward onto his behind — the second person I have ever knocked unconscious. The feeling was euphoric — of being all-powerful — our reptilian inner brain in action.

And now for Alexander Todd. I tracked him down at Mormon Creek, just south of Springfield.

"Alexander Todd," I said to the startled young man atop his riding mule, "you are a dead man."

The business smile disappeared from his lips. "Before you shoot," he said, "hear me out."

"I'm Caesar Honore," I said....

"I know who you are," he said.

I continued: "Not one man in these mountains will raise a finger to punish me when the truth of your deceit is made known."

"The man you want I threw out of my employment when I learned he was unsealing certain letters for a gentleman of your acquaintance," Todd said.

"Zachary Fenner is not a gentleman," I said. "When I get out the word of this business of selling the contents of the private letters of the miners, you will be ruined, if not lynched first.

"Is this man still in these parts?"

"I saw him but an hour ago," said Todd. "He fears the very lynching you suggested for me."

"Does Fenner know he has been caught?" I asked.

"My dealings with this poor creature took place early this morning when we met to exchange mail sacks. I noticed certain letters, all addressed to you, were unsealed. The truth then came pouring out. He's a Christian and this sort of thing unsettled his mind."

"Good," I said, "I have a bit of work for this Christian to perform, work that will redeem his lost soul, and perhaps even return him to his former employment."

Alexander Todd and I sat under an oak tree and composed three letters, in various styles of handwriting.

The first letter was from a "Dr. Timothy G. Littlefield" wondering when he could expect to receive the remodeling plans that would convert the building into a hospital!!!

The second letter was to thank me for getting the seller, Phineas Tremaine (!), to reduce the sales price by what it would cost to repair damage to the busted-out bedroom wall.

The third letter from the same Dr. Littlefield's partner, "Claudius Timberlake, Esq.," expressing regret that I would not be able to continue on as Hospital Grounds superintendent, but appreciated me recommending Mr. Zachary Fenner for the job. They plan to interview him soon as possible. And P.S. They thanked me for recommending the Rev. Owen Lovejoy give the welcoming speech and the benediction when the hospital dedication ceremony takes place.

I confided with Alexander that Lovejoy's fiery speech would probably awaken the dead.

35

Wrapping Up Business

The young ladies were up early.

The Professor had concocted a *bebida especial*.

"This is terrible," said Opal.

"*Mejor la comida de legumbres donde hay amor...*" began the Professor....

Mary Turtle-Eyes finished the Proverb: "...than a stalled ox and hatred therewith."

Gertie gave the citation: "Proverbs fifteen/seventeen."

And Opal the verdict: "This drink tastes more of stalled ox than it does of herbs." The young ladies—even Dandelion who had grown into the role of Mother Superior—giggled.

I was leaving the Vista Del Monte that day.

My work was finished, the property transferred to a soft-spoken, genial miner who had on occasion visited the Vista Del Monte.

In one evening he broke three of Sonora's biggest banks, where the standard wager was a bucket—yes, *bucket*—of gold dust. The miner entered the first bank with a small poke of gold and no friends and walked out with a small fortune and scores of new friends. It took 45 minutes for him to break the second bank and five hours to break the third bank. Sheriff Newton responded to the wild yells emanating from the gambling tents, quickly sized up the situation, deputized two responsible citizens on the spot to act as escorts, and steered the man and his money to a safe harbor.

There Sheriff Newton convinced the new plutocrat to

invest his money in something stable, something that would pay dividends, and something that would give him pleasure. "Have you given any thought to owning a first class whorehouse?" the sheriff asked. The rest is lore.

The young ladies, now five in number, seemed happy and secure. The new landlord, under Sheriff Newton's tutelage, learned the boundaries of his limited role: he owned the building; he did not own the young ladies.

As previously agreed to, the net gain of the Vista Del Monte sale was to be split four ways. I was to receive a quarter, and Burgundia and her two sisters each a quarter. My share came to $5262, not a spectacular boon for the weeks and months that went into this curious enterprise, but sufficient. I was no longer a pauper.

"We have a present for you, Caesar," said Dandelion. Opal stole the show by throwing her body up against me and doing a lewd grating of her pelvis, to the uproarious laughter of her mates.

"Not that kind of present," said Princess. She handed me an envelope. In it was an affidavit attesting to the fact that I acted "honorably" toward the undersigned during our many hours together, and never once did I even hint at "anything improper." It was signed by each young woman and duly legitimized by Sheriff Samuel Newton's official seal.

San Francisco in 1850![190] The great recognized order of society was tumbled topsy-turvy. Doctors and dentists became draymen, or barbers, or shoe-blacks; lawyers, brokers, and clerks turned waiters, or auctioneers, or butchers. Merchants tried laboring and lumping, while laborers and lumpers changed to merchants.

Adventurers, merchants, lawyers, clerks, tradesmen, mechanics and every class in turn kept lodging houses, eating and drinking houses, billiard rooms and gambling saloons, or

---

[190] From start to finish, C. H. is a "borrower." These descriptions of San Francisco are from the *Annals*.

single tables at these. They dabbled in "beach and water lots," 50-*vara* blocks, and new town allotments; speculated in flour, beef, pork, and potatoes; in lumber and other building materials; in dry goods and soft hard and wet goods, bought and sold, wholesale and retail, and were ready to change their occupation and embark in some new nondescript undertaking after two minutes consideration.

The city now had hundreds of rude houses and tents, with hundreds more in the course of erection. All things were in the utmost disorder. Goods and lumber were heaped on streets, passages, and the insides of tents. People bustled and jostled against each other, bawled, railed and fought, cursed and swore, sweated and labored lustily, and somehow the work was done. Horses, mules, and oxen forced a way through, across, and over every obstacle in the streets, and men waded and toiled after them.

San Francisco! So alive! All this plus salt air!

The wedding was elaborate—Hyrum Milton did not know half measures in anything touching on human behavior. He welcomed the guests; he gave away the bride; he performed the marriage ceremony; he blessed the newlywed couple; he signaled Luigi Crespi to bring on the food; he introduced Bayard Taylor, the best man, and his daughter Zinfandella, the maid of honor; he introduced special guests Rick and Scarlet Brazelton; he ordered the music begin for dancing.

Meanwhile in that other world known as Sonora, five fallen priestesses of Vesta, goddess of the hearth, quietly and efficiently went about their business. Like Vesta's Vestal Virgins, they were freed of the usual social obligations to marry and bear children. Like the Vestal Virgins they took a vow, but one that was the direct opposite of the Vestal Virgins' vow of chastity—theirs was a vow to the study and correct observance of giving pleasure to a man to the very core of his existence.

The Vestals became a powerful and influential force in the

Roman state. Five of our young ladies achieved a modicum of that kind of success: Scarlet was a respected business woman in San Francisco; Mary "Turtle-Eyes" Ogilbee owned "Big Mary's Place," Sacramento City's biggest brothel which gave her the means to pull the political strings that controlled the below-board life in the state capital and beyond; Opal married a successful miner and ruled as Queen of the Trinity River; Prudence "Princess" Sharp and her husband owned a chain of hardware stores in the valley; Gertie grubstaked and then married a Russian discoverer of The Burning Moscow Mine in the Mojave Desert region.

We were left with a tragedy and a mystery: Daphne took her own life; Dandelion walked out into the sunlight and disappeared from the face of the earth.

Hyrum made it possible for the good and loyal Professor to send for his family where they prospered on a fruit farm in the Santa Rosa area.

A word of praise for the California setting of my journal: any fool can admire the coastline or the mountains, but it takes a discerning eye to appreciate the great flat valley.

My journal ends here. I avoided the Mexican curse of "May your life be filled with attorneys," but embrace the supposed curse of the Chinese which I find to be no curse at all: "May you live in interesting times."

Living in interesting times teaches us that the best preparation for understanding the things that lie beyond is to understand the things that are at our door.[191]

---

[191] Here C.H. quotes Hypatia, mathematician and neo-Platonic philosopher at the Great Library of Alexandria. He believed, as did Hypatia, that "all formal dogmatic religions are fallacious and must never be accepted by self-respecting persons as final." Hypatia's teachings ran afoul of Cyril, Patriarch of Alexander, who enticed Christian monks to murder Hypatia by flaying her body with sharp oyster shells, as prescribed for "heretics." The Church made Cyril a saint.

About the Author

Eugene L. Conrotto was born in Gilroy, California, at the southern end of Santa Clara Valley known today as Silicon Valley.

He has lived his life two decades at a time.

For the first twenty years he was a student, that experience culminating in a degree in anthropology from Stanford University.

For the next twenty years he was a journalist in the California desert: editor of the award-winning *Desert Magazine*. His first book — *Lost Desert Bonanzas* — came from this experience.

The third twenty years of his life saw him return to the classroom as a teacher. Hence *Classroom Strategies for the Subversive English Teacher*.

The fourth twenty years — and still counting — pretty much confirms Conrotto's belief that the spreading of good cheer is not among his responsibilities.

Conrotto is the author of *Miwok Means People, The Memoirs of Caesar Honore, Classroom Strategies for the Subversive English Teacher, An Annotated Chronology of the California Gold Rush, Notes on My Stay in a Convalescent Hospital, Avanti America, A Day with the Ant-People,* and *A Chronology of Unitarian-Universalist Celebrated Individuals.*

Afterword

I first met Erle Stanley Gardner in Palm Desert in 1960. He came to *Desert Magazine*, a regional publication which I edited, bearing gifts.

The creation of Perry Mason, the fictional lawyer and crime-solver, earned international fame for Gardner. He wrote fiction under a half dozen pseudonyms, and Perry Mason was featured in 80 novels.

But, there was another side to this writer that few of his detective story readers were aware of. Erle Stanley Gardener took great personal pride in his non-fiction writings.

That is the gift he had for *Desert Magazine*: galley proofs of his new book, *Hunting the Desert Whale — Personal Adventures in Baja California*. "Use what you want," he said.

I got three articles from the proofs, all published in 1961: February — *Hunting the Desert Whale — Personal Adventures in Baja California*; April — *Rugged Roads, Whimsical Whales*; May — *Exploring the Virgin Beach*. (All *Desert Magazines* are archived on the web.)

Gardner concentrated his non-fiction writings on three subjects: Travel, Forensic Science, and the subject that became the linchpin that held his suggestion to my novel — Western History. Here's what I remember about Caesar Honore's not-too-immaculate conception….

When I told Gardener I was thinking of leaving the desert and returning to the Mother Lode gold country, he had a suggestion.

Nearly all the '49ers who came to California kept journals. They wrote volumes about the long trip over, but soon as they got here, they threw away their pens and picked up a shovel.

FAKE A '49er JOURNAL: 5% on the ship, 95% roughly divided between the three most exciting places on earth at that time: San Francisco and its Barbary Coast; Monterey where a group of young inexperienced law-makers were writing a Constitution for what would become the richest, most beautiful sub-nation on earth; and Sonoran Camp—the great northern capital of the Aztec people whose blood through the generations will succeed where their knives could not.

SPICE IT UP:

- Have the hero's loving but honest grandson discover the journal long after his grandfather has died, and annotate it—remembering, fixing, questioning, correcting...

- LOVE—Can't have a story without a bit of admiration or even affection.

- PLOT—"You'll think of something."

—elc

Made in the USA
San Bernardino, CA
03 September 2016